A Song for Europe

by

David Mort

1

Published in 2011 by YouWriteOn Publishing

Copyright © David Mort

First Edition

One

The microphone kept cutting out. Pete blinked repeatedly, trying to divert the beads of sweat that were rolling down his forehead. He kept switching the mike from one hand to the other in an attempt to overcome the problem. His gyrations caused several shirt buttons to pop open, revealing a well-developed beer belly.

Gamely, he continued his unequal struggle with the noise coming from the Thursday night crowd in the lounge bar of the Griffin in Toxteth. Most of the drinkers, however, were paying no attention to the singer.

Taking a deep breath, he ploughed on. 'Suddenly...' - he coughed in mid-line, his throat assaulted by the fug of tobacco - 'I'm not half the man I used to be...'

His efforts were interrupted by a bronchial cackle from a buxom woman sitting at a table in a corner of the room.

'Yer wrong there, Pete!' she shouted out. 'With *that* belly, yer *twice* the man yer used to be!'

The woman was in her mid-fifties, her brassy blond hair cut short in a style popular at the end of the nineties. The shade contrasted violently with her lips which were painted the colour of arterial blood.

The people sitting at the next table laughed; one of them shouted called out to her: 'Nice one, Sandra!'

The blonde started to chuckle, too, pleased that her witticism had been appreciated. After rummaging in her handbag, she took out a packet of Benson and Hedges. She usually smoked Embassy Number Six but for nights out with her friends she favoured B and H which she considered to be a more sophisticated brand.

As her laughter subsided, she reached for her drink and took a deep drag on her cigarette.

Suddenly seized by a paroxysm of coughing, she spilled a little of her fourth Bacardi Breezer of the evening. Shaking uncontrollably she dislodged half an inch of ash which fell onto the melamine-surfaced table. The burnt tobacco sizzled for a couple of seconds in a puddle of alcohol before dissolving, adding its own small contribution to the carcinogenic atmosphere of the room.

The singer, meanwhile, undeterred by the interruption, slurred his way doggedly towards the climax of the Beatles' classic.

'Oh, I believe in yes-ter ..'

Eyes closed and hands held together in supplication, he summoned up his energy for the final note. Suddenly the karaoke track came out in sympathy with the microphone and fell silent. The singer stood there, motionless. For several seconds there was total silence until the twenty or so people in the room realised that the performance had come to an end. There was sporadic clapping. Pete raised an arm to acknowledge the applause, revealing a large damp patch on his navy blue denim shirt.

When her fit of coughing had subsided, the middle-aged blonde turned towards the woman sitting next to her. Sandra McNulty had known Maureen O'Dowd since they'd been kids. They were like sisters. They had no secrets from one another. Well, hardly any.

'Thank Christ fer that!' groaned Sandra, lighting up another cigarette. 'He thinks he's bleedin' Paul McCartney! Wadja reckon?'

'Yer dead right there,' said her friend. 'He looks a real sad bastard now, all right. Burr I'll tell yer somethin' fer nothin', Sandra. Back in the sixties he 'ad a smashin' voice. An' he was dead good lookin', too.'

Maureen's eyes misted over as further memories of her teenage years trickled back.

'You remember, don't yer?' she continued. 'All of us gerls was always runnin' after 'im.' She jabbed Sandra playfully in the ribs. 'An' some of us caught him!'

Maureen's recollections continued. 'D'yer remember that biology teacher - what was her name? – yeh, Miss Mulhearn, that was 'er, wasn'it, what used to give us them sex education lessons? She was always tellin' us, in that bloody prissy voice: "There are some things a young lady shouldn't do before sixteen." I remember what you said, an' all, yer cheeky cow! Y'aven't forgot, 'ave yer, Sandra?'

Sandra struggled to remember; it had been a long time ago. She gave up. 'No, it's no good, I can't remember. Wha'd I say, Maureen?'

Her friend giggled. 'You said: "I think yer dead right, miss," - she paused for dramatic effect - "I don't like a large audience, neither!" The old cow was bloody furious! She give yer a whole week's detention for that! It was 'ilarious! I laughed so much I nearly wet meself!'

Sandra chuckled. 'Yeh, I remember it now. It's all startin' to come back to me! An' you know what the funniest thing was? She thought I was jus' bein' cheeky! If she'd've just known what I'd been getting' up to!' She looked at her friend, knowingly. 'An' it wasn't just me, was it?'

That evening Sandra had had a couple of drinks more than usual. Listening to Maureen's anecdote had made her feel nostalgic. She shuffled her tightly-skirted bottom along the green plastic-covered bench seat and moved even closer to her friend. She was about to share a secret that she had kept for over thirty years.

She looked round furtively over each shoulder, like a character in a Les Dawson sketch. When she was satisfied that no-one could overhear, she confided: 'I had 'im once, yer know, when I was fif ... sixteen. He was dead cool. He never said much; he was sort of mysterious, like. 'e 'ad lovely 'air – all black an' wavy, with long sideburns, just like Elvis. An' I'll tell yer somethin' else.'

5

Maureen, curious at the prospect of hearing further revelations, leaned even closer.

''e …'

The precise details of Sandra's reminiscences were drowned out by the amplified voice of Bert, the publican. A former professional boxing referee, he had had many years' experience of seeing people suffer. Grabbing the microphone, he stepped in to save the audience from further punishment. Putting an arm around the singer's shoulders, Bert bellowed: 'Ladies and gentlemen, put your hands together for our very own … Pete Wasserman!'

As the singer stumbled off the stage, Bert slapped him on the back, as he had done many times before to boxers after they had been subjected to a particularly savage mauling.

'Well done, old son,' he said, taking a few moments off from reading In the *Star* about Manchester United's amazing last-minute victory over Bayern Munich in the Champions' League Final in Barcelona the previous night. 'See yer again next Thursday, same as usual, OK?' Bert was already moving back to his position behind the bar.

'When yer ready, pal,' shouted a customer, tapping impatiently on the counter with a two-pound coin.

'Jammy Manc bastards,' muttered Bert, throwing down his newspaper in disgust. The Liverpool FC season-ticket holder angrily gripped the handle of the beer pump and started to pull another pint.

*

Pete emerged unsteadily from the pub into the warm night air. Sweating heavily, he rooted around in his trouser pockets for a handkerchief. His search produced a used tissue, several bus tickets and two further items: a menu from the Indian takeaway just across the road from the Griffin and a crumpled ten pound note.

The discovery of the last two items presented him with a major dilemma: should he buy some cans of lager or pop across the road to the Star of Bengal and get a Vindaloo bum-burner for himself and a chicken korma for his wife, Tina?

Two

Pete had never found it easy to make decisions. In the autumn of 1962, when he was just a kid of seventeen, one of the Fleet Street dailies had sent a young reporter up to Liverpool to gather some background material for a feature the paper was planning to run about the rash of new groups which was erupting onto the Merseyside music scene.

The journalist had watched Pete's group, the Stumblebums, performing at a club in the city. After the gig he asked the four young musicians if they could spare him a few minutes for an interview. Pete's three bandmates hadn't been interested; they had been latched on to by a trio of groupies and had other activities in mind for the rest of the evening. They casually told him to fuck off, before disappearing with their arms around the giggling girls.

Pete had a headache and wasn't in the mood to do the same as the others. He sat by himself in a corner of the room, quietly sipping a pint of Watney's Red Barrel. The journalist came over and sat down next to him, wearing his most ingratiating smile.

'I say, it's Pete, isn't it?' he ventured. 'That's a really, er, groovy sound you chaps have got there!' The reporter's features editor back in London had advised him that a cheery manner and good eye contact were essential if he wanted to win the confidence of the people he was interviewing.

Pete looked up at the oddly-spoken young man, only a few years older than himself, who was grinning broadly at him through black-framed glasses. Pete thought they made him look a bit like Buddy Holly.

'Ta, mate,' said Pete, taking another swig of his pint.

'Allow me introduce myself,' said the stranger, extending his hand. 'The name's Chas Peacock. I'm with the *Daily Excess*. I've come up here all the way from London,' he informed Pete grandly. 'My paper is planning to do a big splash about the really super music that's been coming out of this part of the world recently. I'm thinking of calling my piece "The quality of Mersey." '

He beamed at the young musician, hoping for some sign of appreciation of his play on words. Pete's face remained expressionless; *The Merchant of Venice* had not featured prominently on the English Literature syllabus at his secondary modern school in Toxteth. The man from the *Excess*, undaunted, pressed on.

'Would you mind if I asked you a few questions? You know, just some background details about your group the, er,' - the journalist peered at his notebook over the top of his glasses - 'Stumblebums?'

Pete took a long, slow pull at his drink as he considered this request. Finally, he put down the glass and looked at the young man: 'Yeah, go on then,' he said quietly. Chas, sensing that a promising story was about to unfold, licked the tip of his pencil and opened his notepad.

*

Chas Peacock had graduated from Oxford the previous summer, having barely scraped a third in English Language and Literature. In the months before Finals he had attended interviews with many of the multi-nationals that trawled the nation's universities each year. Not one of these companies had offered him a job. Chas could not understand why. Perhaps, he thought, he had been looking in the wrong direction, career-wise. He decided to seek the advice of the Senior Tutor of his college.

The internationally famous scholar was notorious amongst his colleagues for his biting, sardonic wit. This was lost, however, on all but the very brightest of those at whom it was directed. Chas Peacock was not one of them.

The older man pursed his lips as he focused his powerful intellect on the student's request for guidance.

'Well, Peacock,' mused the Senior Tutor, 'you have several significant attributes which are rare, in my experience, among those who come to study at this ancient seat of learning. Firstly, your essays in tutorials evince an unusually flexible command of the English language as well as a remarkable capacity for coming to conclusions that run counter to all the available evidence; secondly, the degree of importance you so manifestly attach to intellectual integrity has been noted by many of my colleagues as well as by myself; and thirdly, you have, like Caesar, boundless ambition. Taking into account all these factors, it seems to me that a career in the newspaper industry - perhaps a position on one of the more popular organs that shape the opinions of the common man - would be most appropriate for a person with your particular talents. You will undoubtedly go far.' The Senior Tutor looked him directly in the eye. 'At least, I very much hope so.'

Charles expressed his gratitude effusively and left the Senior Tutor's study, fired with optimism. He might have been less cheerful had he ever become aware of what the eminent scholar had said that same evening in the Senior Common Room in response to a query from a colleague.

'Horn-rimmed Herbert?' repeated the Senior Tutor, carefully shelling a walnut with a nutcracker imaginatively designed in the shape of a woman's thighs. 'You are referring, I presume, to that semi-literate, plagiarising, unprincipled little shit, Peacock? There is certainly less to him than meets the eye. I have no doubt whatsoever that he is ideally suited to some sort of menial clerical job on one of the less reputable tabloids. Their attributes would complement one another perfectly. The farther away he goes from this college, the better.' The Senior Tutor smiled thinly. 'That, in essence, is what I told him this morning.'

*

Chas Peacock, greatly encouraged by the Senior Tutor's advice, immediately sent off his CV to the editor of every newspaper in Fleet Street. *The Daily Excess* in particular, with its trademark image at the top of the front page, depicting a knight brandishing a sword in his unceasing quest for truth and justice, had struck a chord with what he imagined the Senior Tutor had said about him.

The editor of the *Excess* was impressed to receive a job application from such a prestigious source. A letter inviting the ambitious undergraduate to attend for interview arrived at his college two days later.

*

The mini-skirted secretary looked no more than eighteen. Teetering on stiletto heels, she smiled at the confident-looking young man as she ushered him into her boss's office. The editor's inner sanctum was smaller than the would-be journalist had expected. It was also extremely hot, due to the output of all three bars on an electric fire that burned incessantly, no matter what the weather.

'Ah, Mr Peacock,' beamed the editor, as he stood up, hand outstretched. 'Do sit down.' He indicated a plastic covered chair in front of his desk, only a few feet from the source of the heat. He turned to his secretary.

'Liz, would you be so kind as to bring us some coffee? Thank you so much.' The younger man's eyes followed her lasciviously as she departed precariously on her mission.

'I hope she remembers to bring some jammy dodgers,' continued the editor. 'They're my favourite.'

Chas Peacock saw an opportunity to ingratiate himself. 'They're my favourite, too,' he interjected. The editor frowned, as if the hoped-for biscuits were for his own and sole consumption.

'Anyway,' he continued, 'let me have another look at your CV.' He perused the poorly typed document for a few seconds.

'I see you are reading English Literature. Now tell me, young man,' he said, peering at the interviewee over the rims of his half-moon spectacles, 'do you consider that your study of late sixteenth century metaphysical poetry would be of any practical value, were I to offer you a position on the *Excess*?'

The younger man had not been expecting such an interrogation. Panicking, he felt a nervous sweat, its effects compounded by the relentless heat from the fire, breaking out all over his body. His drip-dry nylon shirt was sticking to his back and his trousers felt as if they were glued to the plastic chair.

He considered the question in what he hoped the editor would interpret as a studious manner. Finally, he spoke.

'Well, er, I think that, um,' he stammered.

'Yes?' prompted the editor.

At that moment the door to the office opened. The young secretary came back in, carrying a tray laden with cups of coffee which, somehow, she had managed not to spill. As well as balance, she had also shown initiative; on the tray was a plate of her boss's favourite biscuits.

As the editor, momentarily distracted, turned to thank her, the nervous interviewee lifted his bottom in an attempt to break the sweaty bond with the seat. The sound of cloth separating from plastic caused the editor's eyes to turn back from their focus on his secretary. He caught Chas Peacock in a half-standing posture.

'Ah!' he exclaimed. 'Look at that, Liz! Now *there's* something for your I-Spy book - a young man with manners! It's not every day that you'll see a man standing up when a lady enters the room!'

The editor, beaming at Chas, stood up.

'I don't think we need waste any time with taking up references.'

Once again he stretched out his hand across the desk.

'Congratulations!' he exclaimed. 'You've got the job!'

To the astonishment of everyone at his college, Chas Peacock was hired on a month's trial.

*

The tyro reporter distinguished himself from the very start of his probationary period on the *Excess* by demonstrating his ability to brew an excellent cup of tea. The only skill that he had developed during his three years at Oxford, he exercised it frequently in an attempt to ingratiate himself with his new colleagues. It was unfortunate therefore that, as a natural consequence of these frequent tea-breaks, the entire newsroom team was in the gents and so missed the news coming through on the wire services about the death in mysterious circumstances of Marilyn Monroe. The following day the *Excess* had the unenviable distinction of being the only newspaper in the UK not to lead with the story.

The following day the Editor, unaware of Chas's role in the fiasco, decided to give the rookie journalist the opportunity to extend his experience by transferring him to the Features desk. He was sure, he told the young man, that the literary skills that he had acquired during his studies would be put to good use in his new post.

*

Before leaving London to head northwards on his first major assignment, the rookie reporter had spent a few minutes noting down from the latest issue of the *New Musical Express* and *Melody Maker* a list of currently popular Merseyside pop groups. This was going to be rather exciting, he thought, quite a change from his student days, much more fun than ploughing through what everyone else regarded as the great works of English literature.

Chas Peacock had done his homework with the diligence that had made such an impression on the Senior Tutor of his college. The young man from the *Excess* was supremely confident that his feature about the Liverpool Sound would take Fleet Street by storm. Perhaps the piece might even be syndicated and published world-wide. He could see it already: his name, Charles Peacock – the *Excess* disapproved of any abbreviation of their forenames by its writers – would appear in big, bold type at the top of the page. Perhaps, he thought to himself, there would even be a photograph of him, too. He would be famous, rich, in demand. Maybe, one day, he would be awarded – what was it called? - a Pulitzer Prize or something. All he needed, he firmly believed, was just one lucky break.

Three

As the train jerked to a stop at Lime Street station, Chas was determined not to waste a second. He flung open the door of the carriage, jumped down onto the platform and strode purposefully towards the taxi rank. With the self-assurance that went with having an expense account, he instructed the cabby to take him straight to the Cavern Club in Mathew Street. This, he had learnt from his reading of the New Musical Express, was the pop music centre of Liverpool, the place where all the up-and-coming groups on Merseyside could be seen performing every lunchtime as well as each night.

When he arrived at the Cavern just after two o'clock, the place appeared to be deserted. He decided to take a quick look inside. In the dimly lit room a middle-aged woman was cleaning up after the midday session. As his eyes adjusted to the gloom, Chas noticed a poster on a wall featuring a black and white picture of someone he had never heard of, a smiling young man called Tony Sheridan.

On the same poster there was a smaller, slightly blurred image of what he correctly took to be Tony Sheridan's backing group, four scruffy looking characters, all of whom had similar mops of dark hair. Chas decided that they were not worthy of his further attention.

The woman was singing to herself as she propelled a vacuum cleaner around the floor. He recognised the tune. 'My bonnie lies over the ocean,' she warbled. 'My bonnie lies over the sea.' He thought that it was an odd sort of song for anyone to be singing in a pop music club. Every few seconds the cleaner interrupted her vocalising to pick up cigarette packets from the floor, still wet and sticky with the spillage from not-quite-empty bottles of beer.

When Chas Peacock went back outside, the first thing he saw was four youngish lads. He realised after a moment that they were the same ones that he had seen on the poster inside the Cavern. Two of them were leaning against a wall, exhaling clouds of cigarette smoke as they watched the other two struggling to load several big black boxes into a van parked at the end of the street. All four of the youths were wearing matching black suits. Chas thought that their round-necked jackets looked strange without collars or lapels.

He caught a brief snatch of their conversation. 'Hey, George,' said one of them, 'gizza 'and wi' this amp, will yer?'

The youth asking for assistance, Chas noted with distaste, was rather on the short side, with a thick mop of dark hair falling into his eyes and a big nose. There were lots of rings on his fingers. The reporter deduced that these unsavoury-looking characters were the band which had been performing just before his arrival. For a moment he thought about going over and having a word with the one who was wearing the rings, but decided against it. It would be a waste of time and effort; there was absolutely no chance that anyone as short and ugly as that could ever become famous.

It was then that Chas had a brainwave: it would be a really great idea to go up to young people in the street and quiz them about the local music scene. There was nothing, he had been told by a more experienced colleague, like a bit of *vox pop* for helping to get a feel for a place and finding out what really made it tick.

On this occasion, however, his initiative led to an unfortunate incident. When approached by this total stranger who spoke with a strange accent, one young girl, misunderstanding his intentions, started to scream, attracting the attention of a passing policeman. It was only after a lengthy explanation to the highly sceptical bobby that Chas, who had forgotten to bring his Press pass, managed to avoid spending the night as an involuntary guest of Her Majesty.

Later that afternoon the young reporter from the *Excess* saw a poster outside another club, a couple of streets away, advertising a performance by another local group, the Stumblebums, whose name had also eluded his painstaking research. Undeterred by his earlier experiences, he struck up a conversation with a couple of the teenage girls who were queuing to get in.

Were the Stumblebums good, he wanted to know; which one of them did they like the most? Did they think that the group was going to be the next 'Big Thing'? One of the girls looked at her friend before dissolving into an uncontrollable fit of the giggles.

'Big thing? Pete's the biggest. *All* the gerls know that!'

'Bloody teenagers,' muttered the young man, himself barely into his twenties, 'you can never get anything sensible out of them.'

*

Chas brought two pints of draught Bass over from the bar to the table where Pete was sitting. He set the glasses down, managing to spill only a small amount of their contents. All he needed to do now was to ask the young musician the questions he had prepared during the train journey that morning and the information would start to flow. The article, he was sure, would more or less write itself. Pencil poised, he was ready to scribble down the oracular pronouncements from this friendly and obliging member of the next 'Big Thing'. Chas sneaked a final glance at his notepad and pushed his glasses up the bridge of his nose.

After a few routine questions about the other members of the Stumblebums, Chas decided that the right moment had come for him to probe more deeply.

'I get the impression, Pete, that girls find you somewhat enigmatic,' he ventured. 'What do you think the reason for that might be?'

Pete contemplated at some length the contents of his glass.

'You're looking quite pensive, Pete,' prompted the journalist.

The young musician slowly raised his head and looked at him blankly.

'I dunno about that, mate,' he said. 'I'm just thinking.'

Chas Peacock decided that he might have better luck if he were to rephrase the question.

'What I meant to say is, why do you think that so many of your female fans regard you as something of a mystery man?'

Pete's expression didn't change.

The reporter, refusing to be put off by this unpromising start to the interview, decided to try a different approach.

'I've been chatting to some of your fans, Pete. They all agree that you're the most popular member of the group but they say that you're not very decisive. Would you agree with that assessment, Pete?'

The musician considered the question. Chas waited expectantly. Yes! This time he had asked the right question, he could sense it. He could see that Pete was weighing up his response. This could be the moment that would open the verbal floodgates and provide him with all the copy he needed for the feature that would establish his name in Fleet Street!

Slowly, Pete put down his pint and looked at him.

'Am I decisive? Erm, well... yes ... and no.'

The reporter's smile concealed his disappointment; he had heard the joke before. It was obvious that Pete had not.

Chas had no better luck with any of his other questions. Reluctantly, he came to the conclusion that even allowing for a hefty dollop of journalistic licence, he simply was not going to get enough information to develop Pete's laconic responses into a two-page spread for the *Excess*.

'Well, Pete,' he said, finally admitting defeat. 'Thanks a lot.' The irony in the frustrated reporter's voice would have been unmistakeable to anyone else. 'I'll have to be going, now. Don't want to miss my train.'

Pete took another swig of his pint. 'Ta for the drink, mate.'

As Chas emerged from the pub, he reflected gloomily that his journey had been a total waste of time and effort. It was right, what they said in London about there being no civilisation north of Watford. How could anything interesting possibly come out of a godforsaken place like Liverpool? It was obvious that this so-called Merseybeat phenomenon had been grossly exaggerated. The whole thing would be nothing more than a flash in the pan.

He looked at his watch; if he hurried, he could just make it to Lime Street in time to catch the last train back to London.

*

Frustrated by all the time and energy he had wasted, the young journalist vented his spleen in an article in which he lambasted all things Liverpudlian and in particular the musical tastes of the city's young people. Chas Peacock's piece appeared in the *Excess* towards the end of September.

Ten days later, the Beatles released *Love me do*.

Four

The Stumblebums were well named; the four sixteen-year-olds had all left the local secondary modern the previous summer without a single qualification between them. Although not particularly friendly with each other during their time at school, they discovered while serving one of several detentions during their final term that they shared an interest in American pop music. During the summer of 1962, with no work to distract them, they passed the time sharing their enthusiasm for Elvis and Jerry Lee Lewis. That autumn, encouraged by the success of several of their contemporaries whom they considered to be far less talented than themselves, they decided to surf the new musical waves surging out of Merseyside.

The four hopeful musicians, however, caused barely a ripple, failing to stand out from the hundreds of other bands who were doing the rounds on the Merseyside pop scene. The Stumblebums progressed no further than playing a number of gigs on the local pub and club circuit, attracting a small following among some of the local girls who fancied them more for their physical attributes, both visible and rumoured, than for their modest musical endowment.

Don Grant, a camel-coated impresario in his late thirties from Manchester, had heard about the Stumblebums from his married sister Evelyn who lived in Aigburth, one of the smarter suburbs of Liverpool. She told him during one of their regular phone conversations that her fourteen-year-old daughter Sharon was always going on about them. Perhaps, Evelyn had suggested, it might be worth his while to come over and take a look at them.

Grant thought: 'why not?' He had just parted company with another lot of young hopefuls from his home town. He had to admit that, musically, they were quite promising but he had had a major bust-up with them when they would not agree to his inspired suggestion that they change their name to the Ravers. Anyway, he thought, it was their loss; bloody snotty-nosed kids! They would never get anywhere with a damned cissy name like the Hollies.

Grant ventured down the East Lancs road in his Jag. You never knew in this business, he thought; among all the dross he might just be about to unearth a musical gem.

After watching the group perform at a dance hall not far from the city centre, Grant promised the Stumblebums that he would fix them up with a recording session at a studio a few miles from Manchester owned by a pal of his. It would cost him an arm and a leg, he told them. Privately, however, he had a hunch that it would be a tenner well spent.

*

As dawn broke over Stockport one Sunday, the four members of the Stumblebums emerged, sweaty, foul-tempered and exhausted, from a fourteen-hour ordeal in the basement studio. The sour fruit of their labours was just one track that they had managed to get down on tape. It had required thirty-nine takes.

Loving you is all I need, baby, was their attempt at a cover version of a song that had been a minor hit in America a few months previously. The song, Grant predicted confidently, was going to be the Stumblebums' ticket to success. There was just one small problem, he reminded them: they hadn't recorded anything to put on the B-side.

While the other three members of the group had been arguing, between the dozens of aborted efforts, about chord sequences and three-part harmonies, Pete had sneaked into the studio and recorded in a single take a song he had written recently. *Tina* was a simple ballad; he had composed it one day for the one girl he had met who, somehow, was different from all the others. The song featured a solo performance from Pete on vocals and ukulele.

When Pete played it back to the other members of the group, their verdict was unanimous. His song, they said contemptuously, was rubbish. However, as Don Grant had pointed out, they couldn't release a record if it didn't have a B-side. Anyway, he added, what did it matter if Pete's song was no good; after all, no-one ever listened to B-sides, did they?

A few dozen fans on Merseyside bought the Stumblebums' debut disc. It failed however to make any impact at all, nationally, and the group was not invited to record a follow-up. Don Grant disappeared from their lives as suddenly as he had arrived.

Little more than a year after the foursome had first got together, and following a long series of increasingly acrimonious rows, it had become obvious to all of them that they weren't going to make it. After one particularly violent dispute, the Stumblebums disbanded.

*

They had certainly made it, though, during their brief career, with the local groupies. As Pete lurched along in the cool night air, hazy memories of names and faces from over three decades earlier came back to him.

He'd always remember Sheila, a chubby little redhead from Fazakerley; and then there'd been Maggie, a posh bird from Warrington - 'the *good* side of Warrington', he remembered her having insisted. And how could he ever forget – what was her name? – oh, yes, Annie, the sixth-former from the convent; she'd had a long pony tail, a face like an angel and nipples that could poke your eye out if you weren't careful. Unfortunately, he hadn't been careful enough – she had given him his first dose of VD.

There had been quite a few other girls, whose names and faces he would never be able to recall, even when he was sober. But all that had been a long time ago. And then, of course, there was Tina.

Five

The regulars at the Griffin regarded Pete as a bit of a character. He was there most evenings, propping up the bar. Everyone agreed that it was worth the price of a drink just to get him to tell his stories about how, back in the sixties, he had been a rising pop star and best mates with John, Paul and all the rest of the local lads who had gone on to find fame and fortune.

They all egged Pete on, laughing behind his back as he told his increasingly tall tales. Pints appeared in front of him at regular intervals as he recounted the episode about the marathon recording session in Stockport and how on one occasion he had been asked by John to stand in for Paul at a gig in Wallasey when Macca had been feeling unwell. He had had to turn it down, though, Pete informed his smirking audience; he had promised a friend that he would go with him to watch his brother make his début for Everton reserves and didn't want to let him down.

It was a good twenty minutes since the bell for last orders had rung and the lounge bar was emptying. Pete was happy; he had not had to pay for a single drink all evening. And now he had found a ten pound note in his pocket! He was as happy as a pig in shit.

Making his way erratically along the pavement, he reviewed his performance in the Griffin. He could still do it, he reckoned, no problem; he might not be so young these days but the old voice was still holding up OK. He could hardly wait to get home to tell Tina about his success.

The thought that he would soon be back home triggered memories of a sixties classic. 'Ho – ome – ward bound,' he sang, 'I wish I was ... ho – ome - ward bound.' As he wandered past the off-licence and the Indian takeaway, the effort of concentrating on his own, idiosyncratic version of the song had erased from his mind the problem of what to do with the tenner.

Pete's hazy nostalgia for the sixties continued. That was when they'd had *proper* music, he reckoned, like the Beatles and the Stones. And the Yanks, they'd produced some good stuff, too, like Simon and Garfunkel. *That* was great music, not like the fuckin' crap everyone was churning out these days.

Pete's drunken thoughts expressed themselves aloud: 'Fuckin' crap!' His words, directed at nobody in particular, were overheard by a lad who had stopped to light a cigarette and was standing only a yard or two away.

'Yer dead right, there, mate!' said the youth. 'I seen yer in the Griffin just now. You *was* fuckin' crap!'

Pete turned round angrily, unsteady on his feet. 'Yer cheeky little bastard!' he shouted. He lashed out wildly in the general direction of the youth but his flailing arm missed its intended target. Off balance, he stumbled and fell on his face on the pavement. The youth sauntered over and looked down at him, laughing.

'Why don't yer fuck off 'ome, granddad? Yer well past it!'

Pete slowly looked up and tried to get back to his feet. His efforts were interrupted, however, by several pints of the lager he had put down his throat in the course of the evening making an unexpected and spectacularly colourful return journey.

The youth stepped exaggeratedly around the spreading pool of vomit before walking away, slowly shaking his head with contempt. Pete, having finally regained a more or less vertical position, staggered off. Homeward bound.

*

"Home", in Tina's teenage dreams, had meant a four-bedroom semi in Menlove Avenue, one of the posher areas of Liverpool. Her big ambition had been to have a baby to dress up and take for walks in the park in a big Silver Cross pram, and a husband who was a famous pop star. All the girls wanted Pete. But Pete was *hers.*

Most of all, though, "home" had meant escaping from the terraced streets of Toxteth, where she had spent her childhood. She had had to share a bedroom with her two younger sisters who were always screaming at each other. It had driven Tina mad; she had never had a moment to herself. She had never invited her school friends to her house, embarrassed at having only an outside lavvy. It had been bloody freezing in winter.

But all that was going to change when Pete became famous. The Stumblebums were going to go on tours all over the world, and be on television and have lots and lots of hits and they'd be rich! Pete would buy a big American car with enormous fins and chrome bumpers. They'd buy a big telly with walnut-veneer doors like the one she'd seen in the shop window in town and she'd invite all their friends round to watch it. They'd have gas central heating, too, so they'd have hot water *all* the time, and she could have a bath all to herself and she wouldn't have to share it with the other members of her family. And in summer they'd go on a plane on one of them package holidays to Torremolinos - for two whole weeks!

*

Tina emerged from her daydream, sighing heavily as she thought about how things might have turned out. If only ...

She turned off the flickering TV and looked at the clock on the shelf above the gas fire. It was nearly midnight! Where the hell was he? She knew he had gone down to the Griffin because it was karaoke night. He had promised her he wouldn't get pissed. No, love, he had assured her, he wouldn't be home late. He would just do a couple of songs, just to keep in practice. 'Practice for what?' she had asked herself, bitterly. He had never grown up; he still thought he had a future as a singer.

'Pete bloody Wasserman!' Tina spat out the words as if they were a curse. 'Thirty-six years and we're still living in this crappy flat on the same lousy estate!' Her eyes filled with tears of frustration and anger.

*

Mary, Tina's best friend, had persuaded her to go with her to a club in town.

'There's a group on, the Stumblebums,' said Mary. 'I saw them at the Blue Bongo a couple of weeks ago. The drummer's dead fab. D'yer wanna come?'

'Yeh, all right. I've got nutten' else to do,' replied her friend.

Mary's mother, her hair in rollers, stood on the doorstep, looking anxious. 'Make sure you've got enough money for the bus back, gerls! Mind you don't get back too late! Church in the mornin', remember!'

The two sixteen-year-olds skipped down the road towards the bus stop, giggling excitedly. They hadn't heard a word Mary's mother had said.

They got to the club just as the group was coming onto the stage. The four lads all looked about eighteen. They were wearing black suits and white ties that glowed in the dark. Mary, with Tina close behind, elbowed her way forward through the crowd until she reached the foot of the low stage. Mary couldn't take her eyes off the drummer.

'What d'yer think?' she said to Tina. 'Isn't he the dreamiest boy you've ever seen?'

'Yeh, he's all right, I suppose. I reckon that other lad, the one with the bass guitar, is better lookin', though.'

Mary didn't hear her friend's reply. Between songs, he winked suggestively at Mary, slowly sliding his fingers up and down one of his drumsticks. Mary smiled shyly, fluttering her nylon eyelashes. Tina, tapping her feet to the beat, didn't notice anything at all.

At the end of the evening, most of the audience disappeared quickly, heading for their various bus stops. There was no all-night service and for most of them it would be a very long walk home if they missed the last bus.

'Let's go and wait round the back,' said Mary. 'We can get their autographs when they come out and have a chat with them. You never know,' she added with a grin. 'One of them might even ask me out!'

'We haven't got time,' replied her friend. 'The last bus is gonna go, any second, an' yer know what yer mam's like. She'll be frettin' herself stupid.'

'Honest, Tina, you're such a fusspot! We can thumb a lift back. There'll be loads of cars goin' our way. And there *are* two of us, in case you haven't noticed. We'll be all right. Come on. It'll only take a minute.'

'Well,' said Tina, doubtfully, 'if you're sure.'

'Course I'm sure. They'll be right out. Any minute now.'

The two girls waited for about ten minutes outside the back entrance. No-one came out.

'I'm bloody freezing, Mary!'

'Language, Tina! What would your mam say if she could hear you now?'

'Well she can't, and I'm goin' home, so there!'

Just as Tina, in a huff, turned to walk away, the door opened and two members of the Stumblebums emerged. They had changed from their stage clothes into scruffy jeans and polo-neck sweaters. As they struggled to manoeuvre their equipment towards a rusty van, their breath steamed in the cold night air.

'Good crowd tonight, wannit, Billy?' said one of them.

'Yeh, an there was a nice lookin' blonde bird at the front, givin' me the eye all night. She's probably fucked off 'ome by now, though.'

'Yeh, I reckon yer could be right.'

Mary, who had run off to bring Tina back when she'd seen the group coming out of the club, had heard none of this conversation.

'Good job I caught yer, Tina. There they are!'

'About bloody time, too! Well, are we just gonna stand here, or what?'

Mary, trying her best to look cool, walked slowly towards the van. Tina stayed a couple of steps behind her friend. Pete, the lad that Tina had preferred to the drummer, noticed them and carefully put down the amplifier that he was carrying.

'Hello, luv,' he said cheerily to Mary, 'what can I do yer for?'

Mary opened her mouth to reply. She was a fraction of a second too late.

'About a quid, I reckon,' said the drummer.

Mary's eyes filled instantly with tears as she looked in shock at the lad whom, until several seconds earlier, she had really fancied. Furious and humiliated, she turned to Tina.

'Come on, we're goin' 'ome. They're just bloody scallies. If we run we'll make it in time for the last bus.'

Pete turned angrily to Billy. 'Yer a right rotten bastard, you are! She's only a kid!'

The drummer shrugged indifferently and carried on packing away his kit in the van. Pete came over to the two girls.

'Are youse two OK? What's up, blondie?'

'Nutten', I'm fine.' She turned to her friend. 'Are yer comin', Tina?'

'I'll give youse a lift if you want,' offered the young lad.

The girls looked at one another. Their mothers had warned them about this sort of thing, accepting lifts from strangers. But this boy seemed all right, not crude like the other one.

'I'm Pete, by the way, blondie.'

'Yeh, I know. And my name's not blondie, it's Mary.'

'Well, Mary, Mary, quite contrary. D'yer want a lift, then? I don't mean in the van, like. I've got me own wheels.'

'Yeh, all right. I suppose it'll be OK,' said Mary. She turned to her friend. 'Are yer comin', Tina?'

During the drive back to Toxteth, the three of them barely exchanged a word. Finally, Pete asked:

'Where d'yer want droppin', blon ... Mary?'

'Just a couple of streets further on. Just there, that'll be fine, ta.'

'See yer tomorrer,' Tina called out, as Mary got out of the car.

'Yeh, OK,' replied her friend, still angry at what Billy had said.

When Mary had got out of the clapped-out Ford Consul, Pete turned to Tina.

'What's up with her, then?'

'It's your mate, the drummer. Billy, isn't it? Mary really fancied him until he said that ... you know, what he said.'

'He's a fu ..." Pete checked himself. 'He's a bloody idiot, is Billy. His brains is in 'is ... Anyway, he's not my mate. Just 'cos we're in the band together, it doesn't mean we're pals.'

'I suppose not,' she conceded.

'Anyway,' continued Pete, 'I'm not like him.'

'What *are* you like, then?'

'I dunno, really. I've never thought about it.' His face brightened as an idea came to him. 'D'yer wanna find out? I promise I won't eat yer!'

*

Tina hadn't been out with many boys. Quite a few lads had fancied the pretty girl with the long brown hair but were put off by her quiet, serious nature. Tina McGuinness – only her mother called her Christina - had acquired a reputation among the local lads for being hard work. What they really meant was that they didn't have enough patience to get to know her. All they wanted was a quick leg-over. As there were plenty of other girls around who would accommodate them without playing too hard to get, Tina's occasional first date had never led to a second.

'Are you askin' me out, then?' she enquired.

'I suppose I am, yeh!' said Pete. An idea occurred to him. 'D'yer fancy goin' to the pics?'

'Yeh, all right. When?'

'How about next Friday? The group's not playin' or nothin'. If yer like, we could go and see that new James Bond what's on in town.'

Tina remembered Mary's advice about lads. 'Treat 'em mean,' she was fond of saying, 'keep 'em keen!'

Tina, trying her best not to look too interested, turned to Pete.

'Yeh, I don't mind.'

*

Pete and Tina stood for ages in the drizzle outside the Odeon. The uniformed commissionaire looked at them disapprovingly; he seemed to take pleasure in letting older couples jump the queue and go in ahead of them. When Pete and Tina finally gained admission, the main feature had just started. They mumbled apologies as they clambered over the undergrowth of outstretched legs to reach their seats.

As they settled down to watch the film, Tina sneaked a look at Pete. She reckoned that in the near total darkness, if you screwed your eyes up, he looked a bit like Sean Connery. During the next couple of hours, while a succession of beautiful girls succumbed to the

31

charms of James Bond, Tina was impressed that Pete kept his hands to himself and actually watched the film.

As the final credits started to roll, Pete quickly got to his feet. 'Come on!' he whispered to Tina, 'Let's get out quick before *God Save the Queen* starts!'

They made the reverse journey along the row past several tutting monarchists, managing to escape just as the drum roll announcing the national anthem started.

On emerging from the cinema they were pleased to discover that the rain had stopped.

'Look, it's still early,' said Pete. 'D'yer fancy a coffee, like? I know a nice little place. It's just round the corner.'

They sat opposite one another, each warming their hands on a frothy cappuccino. Pete was quiet; he had hardly said a word to her all evening. Still, Tina had to admit that he'd behaved better than most of the other lads she'd been out with. She took another sip of her coffee and looked at him.

'Where d'yer live, Pete?'

'In Huyton. With me Auntie Jeannie.'

'Why don't you live with yer mam and dad? Don't you get on with them, or what?'

'I haven't got a mam and dad.'

'What d'yer mean?'

As soon as she had asked the question, Tina could have kicked herself. Pete looked down at his half-empty coffee cup.

'They're both dead.'

Tina sat open-mouthed, not knowing what to say. She could feel herself blushing with embarrassment. They carried on sipping their coffee, each waiting for the other to speak. It was Pete who finally broke the silence.

'It was two years ago, when I was sixteen. Me mam and dad were goin' into town to do some shoppin'. They were runnin' after a bus and dad … dad had a heart attack. He just dropped down on the pavement. Me mam looked for a phone box to phone 999. She saw one across the road and ran out in front of a car…'

Tina didn't know what to say. She squeezed his hand tightly. Pete continued: 'Afterwards, me Auntie Jeannie took me in. I didn't 'ave no-one else. After we'd paid for the funeral and all that, there was nutten' left. Me mam and dad had never had much. When I went through their stuff … afterwards … I found an old ukulele what I'd never seen him play. I've still got it. I taught meself how to tune it up. I play it sometimes, just to cheer meself up. There was an insurance policy what he'd got to look after me mam in case anything happened to him. That was good, wannit? I got the money when I was eighteen, a few months ago. I spent nearly all of it on the car. Twenty quid, it cost. I reckon I got done - it's knackered.'

He looked up and smiled. 'At least, the ukulele's OK.'

Six

He was a nice lad, was Pete, Tina told her mother; yes, he *was* rather quiet, she agreed, now that you mentioned it, but that was only to be expected, when you took into account what had happened to him. He was quite sensitive, too, thought Tina, not like any of the other lads she'd met. Tina's mother agreed that it was terrible about what had happened to his mam and dad, and how it was so sad that he didn't have a penny and that there was nobody to look after him, apart from his auntie. And yes, she had to admit, her daughter was right; Pete was quite good-looking, too.

Pete had told Tina that he had a job down at the docks; he said it suited him fine because it left him with enough free time to practise with the group and perform when they managed to get a booking.

All Tina's friends were a bit jealous, especially Mary; you could tell by the way they whispered when Tina walked past, holding Pete's hand and laughing. Mary, who had practically lived at Tina's, had stopped coming round to her house. Tina hardly noticed; she had Pete - that was all that mattered. Tina and Pete, Pete and Tina; whichever way she said it, to her it sounded perfect.

*

Over the next few weeks they went out together more and more often. At first it was just on a Friday or

Saturday, depending on which night the group was performing. It was rarely both.

They went to see another show at the Odeon. This time their luck was in; they managed to get seats on the back row. Tina, despite herself, couldn't concentrate on the film.

*

One Sunday, when Tina got back from church, Pete was waiting outside her house in his car, the spluttering of its engine punctuated by an occasional backfiring.

'D'yer fancy goin' fer a drive, like?' he suggested.

Tina tried her best to hide her excitement at the prospect of being driven around. It would make a change from going on the bus.

'Have a good time, Christina,' shouted her mother.

'We will, mam!' she replied, turning her head as the car moved off.

Pete took her for a spin in the Lancashire countryside. It was a fine, sunny day. They stopped at a pub near Preston where they had chicken in a basket.

'What d'yer fancy to drink?' asked Pete.

Tina wasn't sure what to have. She had never touched alcohol - her mother was very strict about the demon drink, as she called it, and had scared her and her sisters with cautionary tales about the fate that awaited those who gave in to the bottle.

Tina had always managed to keep a straight face on these occasions, for the sake of her kid sisters. But her mother wasn't there now and she wasn't a child anymore. Over the bar there was a framed picture of a smiling girl holding up a champagne glass with bubbles coming out of the top. The caption read: "I'd love a Babycham!" Tina, laughing, pointed at the picture and said: *'I'd* love a Babycham!'

'OK, love,' said Pete, and ordered one for her.

When she raised the glass to her mouth, the bubbles went up her nose. Tina sneezed and they both laughed.

When she'd finished the Babycham, Pete asked her if she'd like another one. In the background, the jukebox was playing *Only Sixteen*, a number one hit from a few years earlier. 'She was too young to fall in love,' Pete sang in time with Craig Douglas, 'and I was too young to know.'

Pete and Tina couldn't have been happier if they had been dining at the Ritz. If only every day could be just like today, she thought.

Afterwards, they walked through some fields full of buttercups, their arms round one another's waists.

That warm May evening, Tina arrived home later than usual.

*

'Pete?'

'Yeh?'

'You do love me, don't you?'

'Course I do, yer know that.'

'No, I mean, will you *always* love me?'

'Always, and for ever. Hey, that's not a bad title for a song!'

'Stop it, Pete. I'm being serious.'

'What's up?'

'I'm late.'

'Don't be daft, it's only about ten.'

'I don't mean that! It's … I'm … I'm going to have a baby!'

'Fuckin' hell!'

'What are we goin' to do, Pete?'

'I, er. Well. We'll get married, I reckon.'

Tina burst into tears. 'You don't seem very keen on the idea.'

'No. I mean yeh, really, I am. Let's get married. Tomorrow, if you like.'

'Don't be daft, Pete. We've got no money. How're we gonna manage?'

'Don't worry, luv, we'll be OK. The group's got a few bookings lined up, and there's a guy from Manchester what's been to see us play a couple of times. I think he's an agent, or somethin'. Billy reckons he's gonna gerrus a recordin' contract. We're gonna be big, really big. You'll see.'

Pete put his arms round Tina. She looked up into his eyes.

'We *will* be all right, won't we, Pete?' she asked.

'Course we will, Tina.'

Seven

One day in June, Pete and Tina were married at the Liverpool Register Office in Mount Pleasant. Tina had really wanted the wedding to be on a Saturday but their application, they were told, was far too late. The only available time was a fifteen-minute slot one Wednesday just after the Office opened at nine o'clock.

When Tina had told her mother that she was pregnant, Mrs McGuinness had been heartbroken; as far as she was concerned, the fact that Pete was going to do the decent thing and make an honest woman of her daughter made no difference. She had set her heart on a Church wedding for her eldest child; that was now out of the question.

Too ashamed to look her friends and neighbours in the eye and unable to find solace in her faith, Tina's mother sought assistance from a more terrestrial spirit. Breaking the habit of a lifetime, she took religiously to the bottle.

Apart from Tina's two sisters, nobody else attended the ceremony. Pete's Auntie Jeannie would have been there but she was stuck at home with her leg in plaster. As Tina's sisters were too young to act as witnesses, Pete had to go out into the street to try and find some passers-by who would do the job. Several people ignored his request. It was only when, in desperation, Pete brandished a fiver that a couple of elderly pensioners agreed to oblige.

*

Pete and Tina's wedding breakfast was literally that – a fry-up in a greasy spoon just round the corner from the Register Office. Tina's sisters toasted the happy couple with mugs of stewed tea before going off to school. Together, they had worked out their excuse for being late: they would tell their teacher that they had had to take their dog to the vet's because he had been very ill in the night. The vet had said it was cancer and it would be for the best if he put the poor creature to sleep. The girls knew that their teacher, a grey-haired grandmotherly lady, had a dog of her own so she would be sympathetic.

When Pete and Tina returned to where he had left the car, they found a traffic warden sticking a parking ticket under the Consul's windscreen wipers. Pete tried to explain that he and Tina had just got married, but no amount of pleading would make the woman relent. Tina burst into tears; it wasn't a good start to their new life together.

Pete and Tina spent their first night as a married couple in the box-room of a cheap boarding house in Southport. In Victorian times the seaside resort had been very up-market. Today, over half a century later, it was beginning to look somewhat down at heel but striving to preserve an air of respectability.

Pete hadn't booked anywhere for them to stay; forward planning was not his strong point. Even though the holiday season was not yet in full swing, all the guest houses on the sea front had "No Vacancies" signs in the window. He had been told by one of his mates that there was quite a nice place in Bank Square, just off the promenade, but when he phoned to enquire whether there were any vacant rooms, it turned out to be fully booked, too. Even in the small bed and breakfasts, there was not a room to be had.

After searching for three hours, they came across a narrow terraced house which displayed a "Vacancies" sign in the window. The dirty net curtains made it impossible to see inside *Seaview,* which was situated several hundred yards from the sea front.

The sky had turned grey and it was starting to drizzle. Pete rang the bell on the door on which the brown paint was flaking away. He had to ring several times before it finally opened. The woman who stood before him looked as if, in a previous incarnation, she might have been in charge of executions at Holloway. She was unimpressed to learn that the couple was intending to spend only one night under her roof and her grim expression made it clear that she had reservations about their marital status. The fact that all the young couple had by way of luggage was a small holdall served only to confirm her suspicions. She ran a *respectable* establishment, she informed them.

Tina and Pete looked at one another, thinking that they should try to find somewhere else. But it was getting late and their chances of finding another place to spend the night were not good. Although they felt angry and humiliated, they said nothing. The landlady's commercial instincts, however, triumphed over her moral principles. She gestured in the direction of the staircase.

'The only room I've got free at the moment is up there, on the third floor. There's a toilet on the landing below. The lock's broken. You'll have to whistle when you, you know, pay a visit.' There was no trace of humour in her voice. 'Breakfast is from seven-thirty till eight-thirty,' she informed them. 'And make sure you're out of the room by nine o'clock sharp, otherwise I'll have to charge you for a second night. *Seaview* is very popular, you know; you're very lucky I can fit you in.'

The box room at the top of the house was barely wide enough for the double bed. The springs squeaked when Pete sat on the lumpy mattress.

'I think there's a mouse in there!' he joked. Tina was not amused. The floor, covered with a dark brown, threadbare carpet, was uneven and the creaking door of the utility wardrobe kept swinging open, despite Pete's attempts to jam it shut.

Later, as Pete snuggled up to her, Tina suddenly sat upright.

'Pete!' she whispered. 'I can hear someone outside the door! I bet it's her. She's checking up on us, the old cow! I *knew* she wouldn't believe you when you told her we'd just got married. Oh, Pete! This place is *horrible*!' Tina burst into tears again. Pete tried to put his arms around her but his bride, sobbing, shook her head and pushed him away.

The newly-married couple spent the rest of their wedding night staring at the cracks in the ceiling and the peeling wallpaper. As dawn broke, they watched the watery sun come up through the gap between the faded, unlined curtains.

When Pete and Tina came downstairs they were surprised to see that there was nobody else having breakfast. The landlady commented sarcastically on how exhausted they looked. Roughly banging down a metal teapot on the table in front of them, she muttered something about morals and rabbits. Some of the teapot's stewed contents spilled onto the already stained tablecloth.

Hardly looking at one another, Pete and Tina ate their corn flakes and drank their tea in silence. The undercooked breakfast was cold. They left it untouched. Pete fished out a five pound note from his pocket and paid the woman who stuffed the money into her grubby pinafore without a word of thanks.

Standing grim-faced on her doorstep with her arms crossed defiantly across her chest, like a footballer in an ancient team photograph, she watched the newly-weds depart. As the Consul moved away, the front door of *Seaview* slammed shut.

Eight

Pete and Tina started their married life in the spare room of Pete's Auntie Jeannie's council maisonette. The old lady had been widowed many years earlier and didn't have any children of her own. She was very fond of the young couple and did her best to be as unobtrusive as possible. Everything was fine during the day, but at night … The wall between their bedroom and hers was so thin that Pete reckoned you could have heard a moth fart on the other side.

The couple's worldly possessions were few; they had bought a second-hand double bed that they'd seen advertised in the local paper - the stains on the mattress appeared to be nothing more unpleasant than tea. They had also acquired an ancient sofa that a friend of Tina's mother had given them to save her the trouble of taking it to the tip. Finally, to complete the picture of domestic bliss, they had a shop-soiled record-player which they'd got for peanuts in a sale. The barely-portable Dansette had a couple of dents in the casing and needed a new sapphire needle.

Pete and Tina went to the Town Hall to put their names down on the waiting list for council accommodation. They were informed by an official with a grubby collar that it would be at least three, possibly four years before they would have any chance of being considered for a one-bedroom flat.

'You simply don't have enough points, you see,' said the man.

'Like Everton, yer mean?' asked Pete. The official didn't smile. It didn't matter; Pete hadn't been making a joke.

In spite of everything Pete and Tina didn't have a care in the world; they were in love and, as far as Tina was concerned, nothing was ever going to change that. Every evening when Pete came home to Auntie Jeannie's after work, he would kiss his wife and gently stroke her growing bump. Sometimes, when he wasn't feeling too tired, he would pick up his ukulele and serenade her: 'Just Tina and me,' he sang, 'and baby makes three, we'll be so happy in my blue heaven.' Soon, when the baby came, they'd be a proper family, just like in the song.

*

Two months later, after a bust-up between Billy, the drummer, and the other members of the group, the Stumblebums disbanded. Billy, disillusioned with pop music, smashed up his drum kit in a violent rage. When he calmed down, he decided to carry on with his day job as a furniture remover. The two other lads, Dean and Jimmy, sold their guitars and amplifiers to an even younger quartet of musical hopefuls. With the proceeds the two lads bought a small van, a ladder and bucket and started up a window-cleaning round on a housing estate which had recently gone up. As for Pete, he was quite happy to carry on working at the docks.

*

Late one drizzly afternoon, Tina was running to catch the post with their weekly pools coupon when she caught the heel of her shoe in a crack in the pavement. She fell heavily. A small crowd of passers-by gathered around the pregnant girl.

'Y'all right, luv?' enquired an elderly man.

'It's OK,' she managed to say, even though she was in a lot of pain. 'I'll be all right. I don't think I've broke nutten'.'

Although badly shaken, Tina felt more embarrassed than injured. One of Auntie Jeannie's neighbours who happened to be passing escorted her home.

In the middle of the night, Tina woke up in agony. When Pete put the light on, he was shocked to see blood all over the sheets. He ran out to the phone box on the corner of the street to ring for an ambulance.

At the hospital, Tina was attended to immediately and was reassured that she had not sustained any serious injuries. The doctors, however, were unable to save the baby.

Nine

The scraping sound of the key as Pete tried to locate the front door lock announced his return from the pub. Not wanting to wake Tina, who would certainly be asleep at this late hour, he cursed quietly as he stumbled along the hallway. In the living room a dim light was still on.

Pete was amazed sometimes that Tina had stuck with him all these years. They had been shocked when the doctors had told her she would never be able to have another baby. They had never really explained why and both of them, too intimidated to question their professional opinion, had accepted it. Tina and Pete never spoke about it again and Pete thought she seemed to get over it eventually. She didn't give him too hard a time about his drinking, either. She was all right, was Tina.

He opened the door and went into the living room.

'Where the hell have you been till now?' demanded his wife.

'Down the Griffin,' he slurred. 'Had a great time. Jussad couple o'drinks. Done a few songs, too.'

The memory of his musical exploits at the pub was rekindled as he launched into a repeat performance of *Yesterday*.

'The old magic's still there!' he exulted. 'I've still gorrit!' He stretched out his arms towards his wife. 'I love you!' he declared passionately. 'Gizza kiss, you gorgeous girl!'

Tina pushed him away in disgust.

'Look at the state of you! You're disgusting. You stink of beer and puke. Get away from me!'

'Don't be like that, Tina, doll. I love you. Look! I've got some money!' he said triumphantly, brandishing the crumpled ten pound note in the air. 'I'll buy you anything you want.'

'Don't think you're getting round me like that,' shouted Tina. 'You're nothing but a drunk and a waster. You can't keep a job for more than five minutes! It's no bloody wonder we're still stuck in this dump!'

Tina moved towards her husband, jabbing him fiercely in the ribs with an index finger. She was in full flow.

'You spend all your time in that bloody pub, drinking yourself stupid. We've barely got enough money to pay the bills as it is. You go from one dead-end job to another and you haven't saved a penny! If it wasn't for what I bring in each week from Tesco's we'd be living on benefits. And just tell me this: how do you think we're going to manage when we're old, eh? Have you ever thought about that? Have you hell! I wish to Christ I'd never set eyes on you!'

Having finally run out of steam, she turned her back on him, her arms folded.

Pete had heard it all before - many times. His usual response when Tina went off on one of her tirades was to get out of the flat and escape to the sanctuary of the Griffin. It wasn't that he wanted a drink, necessarily, but being out of the way for a while gave her time to calm down. She always came round in the end. It was probably something to do with her age. He'd heard that women often went a bit funny when they were getting on for fifty. Strange buggers, women, he thought to himself; no matter what you did, they were never happy.

This time, though, he could sense that Tina's ranting was more venomous than usual.

'Tina, luv, just listen a minute,' he pleaded. 'I wanna tell yer somethin' - somethin' important.'

'What?' She didn't turn round. Pete opened his mouth to speak, but no words emerged. Instead, his eyes went glassy, his mouth fell open and the remainder of the lager he'd drunk that evening cascaded onto the carpet.

He sank to his knees then slowly looked up, helplessly. Tina turned round and looked down at him, then at the spreading pool on the threadbare carpet. Her expression hardened. When she finally spoke, her voice was unusually calm.

'That's *it*. I'm leaving you, Pete. I should've done it years ago.'

Tina slowly went up the stairs, leaving Pete on his knees, looking down in bewilderment at the stinking mess he had produced. A few minutes later, she came down, carrying a suitcase. Without a word, she walked past her husband, opened the front door and closed it quietly behind her.

Ten

A detailed knowledge of European geography as well as exceptionally acute eyesight is required to locate Slavonicia on a map. A tiny, mountainous and landlocked country with a population of fewer than two million, it is situated many hundreds of miles from Moscow, its former master. In contrast to the fertile and fossil-fuel rich lands by which it is surrounded, Slavonicia's stark, forbidding terrain is not favoured, according to the encyclopaedias, with any commercially viable natural resources.

In the early Middle Ages, a succession of plundering tribes from the East had taken one look at the bleak landscape and, having decided that there was nothing there that was worthy of further investigation, had continued relentlessly in the time-honoured pursuits of looting, raping and pillaging. The invaders had settled finally in the Carpathian basin where they had laid, in addition to the women, the foundations for what would become, centuries later, the Austro-Hungarian Empire.

In a much more recent period of history, even the rapacious land grabbers of Nazi Germany had also, uncharacteristically, shown no interest in laying claim to this desolate land. Consequently Slavonicia, unlovely and unloved, continued its unremarkable existence as the Cinderella of Eastern Europe.

In 1945, after the end of the Second World War, the USSR, less fastidious than the sensitive souls of the Third Reich when it came to extending its empire, annexed the impoverished territory and introduced to its meagre population the delights of a system of government untainted by the evils of capitalism.

Established in 1992, following the disintegration the previous year of the USSR, the fledgling democracy of Slavonicia was finding it a struggle, after decades under communism, to come to terms with the more liberal values of the free world. Even in the highest échelons of government, there were still those who secretly regretted the demise of the former régime. More than one Minister looked back with nostalgia to the good old days when the smack of firm government had been applied, often quite literally, to those few brave souls who had had the temerity to question the wisdom of those in power.

Today, the country was the hapless butt of the cruel joke of bigger, wealthier countries. The desperate poverty of the People's Independent State of Slavonicia was accurately encapsulated in its acronym.

*

At the weekly meeting of the Council of Ministers, the President of Slavonicia was addressing his Cabinet. His mood was sombre. Normally a private man who seldom displayed his feelings, he was unable to conceal on this occasion the powerful emotions which were welling up inside him.

'Comrades - I beg pardon, old habits die hard – brothers, I need hardly remind you of the economic difficulties which are sapping the morale of our fellow citizens and which threaten the economic and political stability of our nation.'

He paused before delivering the first blow.

'The failure of the beetroot crop, for the first time in living memory, has brought our people to the very brink of starvation. Our repeated requests for foreign aid have fallen on deaf ears.'

His voice was now tinged with bitterness.

'As we have neither oil nor mineral deposits, we are obviously of no interest to the Western powers which, despite their fine words, ignore those countries that are unable to offer them any return on their investment.'

He paused for a few seconds to regain control of his composure. Nobody dared to interrupt. The President continued.

'But it is not the shortage of food that constitutes the most urgent threat to our glorious nation; there has occurred today a catastrophe of even greater significance. My brother ministers, Slavonicia now faces an unprecedented crisis, one so grave that it could well lead to the downfall of our government.'

The collection of grey-haired, middle-aged men around the table stared in shocked silence at their leader. What, they wondered, could possibly be worse than the failure of the beetroot crop?

The President paused theatrically before dropping his bombshell.

'It is with profound sadness that I have to inform you that our national football team has been eliminated, in the most scandalous circumstances, from the qualifying competition for the next World Cup.'

A gasp went up from the members of the Cabinet. What – they wondered - were the scandalous circumstances to which the President was alluding? Had one of the players failed a drugs test? Had the team manager's attempts to bribe the match officials, a procedure carried out on a number of previous occasions with total discretion, been discovered? Whatever the reason for the team's elimination from the competition, it was indeed, as the President had said, of crisis proportions; in Slavonicia, football was the national obsession.

'I shall now read to you an extract from our own official observer's match report,' continued the President. He cleared his throat before assuming a sombre tone: "Slavonicia's heroic players held out bravely for three whole minutes against the Faroe

Islanders, who had resorted to intimidatory tactics and outrageous gamesmanship direct from the kick-off. Had it not been for eight controversial goals shamefully allowed by the referee, who was quite clearly in the pay of the opposition, our valiant national team would surely have gained a thoroughly merited place in the playoffs."
'

The President put down the single page report and surveyed, over the top of his dark-tinted glasses, the stunned expressions on the faces of the members of his government. 'Brothers,' he declared, 'there can be no doubt concerning the absolute accuracy of what I have just read to you. I have received it directly from the head of the Slavonician Headquarters for Information and Tourism. He is a man who is not given to exaggeration or to distortion of the truth and I hold him in the highest regard.'

The President paused again and looked at the assembled ministers. 'Brothers,' he continued, 'I am sure that you are as aware as I am of the depressing effect that this outrageous and wholly undeserved def... injustice will have on the morale of our fellow-citizens. It is therefore a matter of the greatest urgency that we discover a way to create what I believe they call in the West a "feel good factor". I need hardly remind you that the next general election is due to be held less than a year from now. If our government should be defeated,' he added tartly, 'we shall *all* find ourselves eating cabbage soup and beetroot – always assuming that there is any available. Consequently, I shall be pleased to hear your suggestions as to how we can avoid political and economic disaster.'

The members of the Cabinet, still shocked by their leader's revelation, broke into clusters of twos and threes, whispering animatedly. The noise level rose rapidly until it became deafening. The President, considering it beneath his dignity to shout in order to be heard above the din, took off one of his elegant, highly-polished Oxford brogues and banged it several times on the no less deeply burnished mahogany table. This unconventional step achieved the desired objective, bringing the ministerial team to heel.

The President, now that the meeting was once more under his control, returned to the subject he had raised. Among the men seated around the table, he knew that there was one above all to whom he could turn in a crisis, confident that he would produce a solution to whatever problem might be facing the government. His other ministers, reflected the Head of State, presented him only with problems; the man to whom he now turned was unique: he provided solutions. The President looked at him and smiled.

'Brother Secretary Nudnik, my trusted colleague and friend, what do you propose that may enable us to respond to the present situation?'

Dr. Nicolai Nudnik, the Controller of the National Treasury, was a short, slightly built, former teacher of mathematics. Several years previously he had presented his doctoral thesis on deficit management in the political economy. The ideas expounded by Nudnik, in what had been hailed by his peers as a seminal work, had come to the attention of the President. He had been particularly impressed by the ingenious stratagem advanced by the young academic.

In the conclusion to his thesis Nudnik had proposed that any person suspected of being a political activist and a potential threat to the government should be arrested and charged with offences against the State. Then, after a scrupulously fair trial - held regrettably, but inevitably, given the security implications, *in camera* – such persons would be sentenced to a lengthy term of imprisonment. Invariably, following the successful appeal by the condemned against both conviction and sentence, they would receive a token amount of compensation, an *ex gratia* payment made without any admission of guilt on their part by the authorities.

However – and here was Nudnik's stroke of genius – the State would immediately counter-claim for the cost of the detainee's accommodation, food, prison clothing, recreation and supervision, not merely for the period of incarceration already served, but for the duration of the entire sentence. Almost all of these political activists, Nudnik had maintained, belonged to the country's small but relatively wealthy intelligentsia, and could afford to pay. Pragmatically, they did so rather than risk being re-imprisoned for non-payment. The small minority who possessed insufficient funds would be sentenced to an even longer term of imprisonment with hard labour – thus providing the State with free manpower.

The argument advanced by Nudnik in support of what, to the uninitiated, might have appeared to be an indefensibly absurd and outrageous slap in the face of natural justice, was that the State had incurred forward expenses in planning for the long term incarceration of such detainees. By counter-claiming, the State was merely seeking to recoup the costs to which it was committed. In each case, the sum claimed by the State would far exceed the amount paid in recompense to the unfortunate victim.

Nudnik's fame had spread. A number of foreign governments, both in Europe and beyond, had shown an interest in adopting the ideas of this indisputably original thinker. It was rumoured that he had been offered large sums of money if he would care, purely in the interests of academic research, to lend them his expertise.

The President knew that such talented individuals, just like footballers, had their price and that he would have to act quickly if he was not to run the risk of losing the services of this exceptionally brilliant man.

Shortly thereafter, Nudnik had been plucked from provincial obscurity and appointed as Special Adviser to the Finance Minister. A short time later, following the sudden death, apparently of a heart attack, of his immediate superior, Nudnik had been the natural choice to succeed him.

*

Nudnik removed his round rimless glasses and with great care polished the lenses. The President and the rest of his colleagues waited eagerly for him to reveal to them the path to salvation.

Who among them could forget his notion only a couple of years earlier of getting the State to provide, absolutely free of charge, unlimited quantities of 100º proof beetroot liquor to all citizens who had been diagnosed with early stage cirrhosis of the liver? As there had been a beetroot glut that season this breathtakingly original measure had been achieved at virtually no cost to the State.

As well as bringing mind-numbing relief from their misery to the increasing numbers of the nation's alcoholics, Nudnik's brainwave had relieved pressure on the country's overstretched health service. As the drinkers began to die in their hundreds, there was a corresponding reduction in the numbers of those waiting for hospital treatment.

Nudnik's inspired idea had brought many further benefits for Slavonicia; cohorts of able-bodied men and women had been recruited by the State Forestry Department to chop down trees from which to make coffins and more labourers had been needed to dig graves for all the newly-deceased dipsomaniacs.

Hundreds more had found employment in the State-run quarries, cutting out huge slabs of granite of which, thanks to the mountains which encircled the country, there were inexhaustible supplies. The blocks of stone, in turn, were delivered by an expanded State-run transport service to monumental masons, who were now experiencing an unprecedented demand for their skills in crafting memorials to the dear departed.

The only group of workers which had not benefited from Nudnik's plan had been the embalmers; the subjects on which they practised their cosmetic arts were already deeply pickled and required no further preservative measures.

These innovative socio-economic measures had caused a considerable stir internationally. It was even rumoured that the United Kingdom's government, its socialist-inspired National Health Service also chronically plagued by financial difficulties, had been so impressed by Nudnik's scheme that it had sent a working party to Slavonicia, in what the entire British press had reported were conditions of total secrecy, to consult with the creative visionary who had proposed them. There was no doubt that, on days such as this, Nicolae Nudnik had demonstrated his stature as a man of genius.

Today, however, was not one of those days. Nudnik scratched his bald head, pushed his glasses up with a forefinger from the end of his nose and sighed deeply.

'Mr. President, I fear that, in the present circumstances, we appear to have no alternative but to adopt traditional methods to solve this difficulty. Our only course of action is to approach the International Monetary Fund for assistance. Having studied the latest information provided by my department, I estimate that we shall require a loan of' – Nudnik took out of his jacket pocket a calculator and tapped it for several seconds – '10 billion US dollars. This would buy us time, at least until after the election. Once the loan was agreed, we could announce immediately massive popular – and of course vote-winning – measures, such as cuts in income tax, a reduction in the five-year waiting time for the purchase of private vehicles from our automobile factory, and even' - the Minister's voice rose as he became increasingly excited by his vision - the removal of the surcharge on families which produce more than one female child. The people will ...'

The President, whose facial expression during his protégé's peroration had gradually changed from confident expectation to crimson-complexioned fury, cut the Minister short.

'Have you taken leave of your senses, Nudnik? This is total lunacy! What you are proposing would lead inevitably to economic ruin for Slavonicia. The State

Treasury would never be able to afford the interest charges on such a loan, to say nothing of repayment of the capital.'

The rest of the Cabinet remained silent. Having witnessed the merciless demolition of the man who, until a few moments earlier, had enjoyed the absolute respect of the President, they were reluctant to contribute any ideas of their own for fear of being similarly humiliated. The President, his hopes of economic salvation dashed, was now slumped in his seat, his head in his hands.

A few moments later the gloomy silence was interrupted by a polite cough. The person responsible was Mikael Shashlik, the recently appointed Minister for Arts and Popular Culture and by far the youngest member of the Cabinet. A brilliant linguist and economist, he had graduated top of his year at the State University.

This idealist with an original cast of mind had been attracted by a career in teaching. Six months into his first – and, as it proved to be, his only – teaching post, his sense of pedagogic vocation had been stretched to breaking point as he discovered to his despair that few of his young charges shared his idealistic notions about education.

When the Government had sought his services, Shashlik had been only too ready to accept. The honour of serving his country was, he felt, far greater than that of attempting to teach English to a rabble of uninterested teenagers. His decision had in no way been influenced by the fringe benefits attaching to his new post – a Russian-style country *dacha,* an official car and driver and, not least, frequent research trips abroad – which came with his new position. He particularly enjoyed the regular fact-finding trips to Colombia; the visits to the production facilities near Medellín were extremely stimulating.

Shashlik coughed again. 'Mr. President,' he said, 'may I offer a suggestion?'

The President, frowning, looked up.

'By all means, brother Shashlik; whatever you have to say can surely be no more imbecilic than what has already been proposed.' He glared again at the disgraced Nudnik, who was slumped in his seat, a broken man.

Shashlik, undaunted by the verbal savaging to which his senior colleague had been subjected, spoke up with the confidence of youth.

'Mr. President, I believe that in our present situation conventional measures such as those suggested by my esteemed colleague' – his eyes turned momentarily to the inert, ashen-faced Nudnik – 'would be entirely useless. We need to find a new way of addressing this challenge. If I may be permitted to use an American expression, it will be necessary to think outside the box.'

'Box? What box? What the devil is he … ?' demanded testily another Minister, a relic of the previous régime who had been retained as a sop to the more traditional elements of the electorate. The President slammed his fist on the table.

'Be quiet, Bogashvili! I do not recall that *you* have made any useful contribution to this meeting!'

The President's anger subsided as quickly as it had flared up. He turned his head toward the young Minister. 'Brother Shashlik,' he smiled encouragingly, 'please continue.'

'Thank you, Mr. President. As I was saying, we must find a way to distract the attention of the Slavonician people from our present difficulties.'

'Yes, yes, Shashlik,' interrupted the President, peevishly. 'Our distinguished colleague' – he shot another withering glance at Nudnik – 'has already offered us the benefit of his wisdom in that regard. Do you have something more sensible to propose?'

'With respect, Mr. President, I believe that what I am about to suggest may provide the solution to the current situation.'

'Very well,' snapped the President, 'get on with it!'

'Of course, Mr. President,' responded Shashlik, meekly. 'What I propose is that Slavonicia ... win the Eurovision Song Contest!'

The President stared incredulously at the young man but before he could vent his anger at this clearly absurd idea, Shashlik enthusiastically forged ahead.

'Mr. President, brother Ministers, I would ask you to consider for a moment the logic of what I am proposing. If Slavonicia were to win the Eurovision Song Contest, it would, literally and metaphorically, put our country on the world stage. Slavonicia would be invited, according to long-established tradition, to host the event the following year. Massive sums of money would flood into our national Treasury from television and radio broadcasting rights, as well as huge revenues from international advertising, not to mention sales of CDs and video recordings of the event.' Shashlik paused before playing his trump card. 'In the longer term, the publicity generated by Slavonicia's success would add considerable weight to our nation's bid for membership of the European Community.'

'Bid? What bid?!' spluttered the Foreign Secretary, another member of the old guard who still viewed the West with deep suspicion.

'A bid, Brother Foreign Secretary,' responded Shashlik, unperturbed, 'which, if successful, would guarantee the future economic prosperity of Slavonicia - for all time!'

Immediately, there was uproar. Nudnik, deflated a few moments earlier by the President's withering criticism of his original proposals, was now encouraged to find his voice again on hearing Shashlik's plan. The usually mild-mannered scholar erupted.

'This is ludicrous! Outrageous! I have never heard such an idiotic suggestion! Has this pipsqueak taken leave of his senses? He has been a member of this government for five minutes and already he is proposing measures that will bring down further ridicule and shame upon our nation.'

Shashlik, in the face of this torrent of abuse, remained perfectly composed.

'Brother Minister,' he began, directing his mild gaze towards Nudnik, 'with all due respect to your seniority and many years of experience, I believe that I have a better appreciation than yourself of our people's cultural preferences.'

He turned to his leader.

'If I may speak frankly, Mr. President – and, please believe me, this is not intended as a slight on the valuable efforts made so far by any of my esteemed colleagues – our fellow citizens are no longer willing to endure the poverty to which they have been subjected for far too long.'

Shashlik warmed to his theme. 'Man cannot live on beetroot alone!' he declaimed. 'Our people hear about the standard of living in the West and, quite understandably, they are envious. They perceive that the advent of democracy, despite its many benefits, has brought no improvement to their daily lives. Our citizens are downcast, defeated, without hope. Such public sentiment, if it is allowed to fester, could lead to unrest, violent demonstrations, even to civil war. But, Mr. President and distinguished colleagues, if' - Shashlik paused for effect - 'if Slavonicia could achieve a success of this nature it would, I believe, restore national morale overnight and, with the assistance of the generous subsidies provided by the European Community to its less privileged members, guarantee the economic and social benefits to which I have alluded.'

The President steepled his fingers and pondered. The entire Cabinet watched him in nervous silence. Finally, their leader spoke.

'Your idea certainly has the distinction of being original, brother Secretary. But there is something of which, I suspect, you may be unaware.' The President paused as he recalled the awful event that had occurred several years earlier and to which the Foreign Secretary had referred. Shashlik knew better than to interrupt. He did not have to wait long in order to be enlightened.

'Following the liberation of Slavonicia from the repressive yoke of communism, our government was persuaded by the then Minister for Arts and Popular Culture to celebrate our country's independence by taking part in the self-same Eurovision Song Contest which you propose that we enter.'

The President's expression clouded over at the memory of that fateful chapter in the annals of Slavonicia.

'What followed was without doubt one of the darkest days in the history of our nation; the ignominy to which we were subjected remains to this day a festering sore on the national psyche.'

Shashlik knew better than to quibble with his President's occasionally wayward use of language. He did not want his own psyche – or, more realistically in view of the country's history of violent repression, his body – to acquire any sores, whether festering or otherwise. He waited patiently for his leader to continue.

'As each country cast its votes,' continued President Sonofábic, 'it became increasingly clear that our glorious nation was being slighted, insulted, humiliated. The song that had been entered on behalf of Slavonicia was awarded not a single vote!' The President's voice shook with anger. 'Not – one – solitary - vote!'

The President, struggling to regain his composure, looked at Shashlik.

'It may be, brother Secretary, that you are unaware of the fate that befell the composer of our country's entry for the contest?'

Whether or not the question was intended to be rhetorical, Shashlik had no opportunity to discover. The President looked at the high ceiling of the Cabinet Room as he proceeded to recount the tragic aftermath of Slavonicia's day of shame.

'The man who brought disgrace on our glorious nation was a Professor of Physics at the State University, here in Bograd, where you yourself were a student, I believe. His favourite pastimes,' continued the President, 'when not engaged in failing to make scientific discoveries, were to play the balalaika – which he did, I am informed, extremely badly - and also attempting to write popular songs. He was invited by your predecessor at the Ministry for Arts and Popular Culture to compose an entry for that year's Eurovision Song Contest.'

The President's features took on a suitably sombre expression.

'Not long after the débâcle of that evening, further tragedy struck when the Minister was killed in a hit and run incident. Despite an extensive investigation to bring to justice those responsible for this heinous crime, no-one was ever apprehended. As for the Professor, he was invited to take part a few weeks later in an international Physics symposium in Bulgaria. At the end of the official proceedings a banquet was held to celebrate the success of this prestigious event. It seems that, after the main course, he called for a toothpick, as was his custom. A packet of them was brought to him by a young waiter. It was reported that a few seconds later, the Professor suddenly stood up, clutching his throat and gasping loudly. According to those who witnessed this shocking scene, his face turned blue and he collapsed across the table, shattering two full bottles of a rather exceptional Châteauneuf-du-Pape. It was a terrible irony that, among all the eminent doctors present, not a single one possessed any medical qualifications. Not that a doctor would have been of much use - the Professor was already dead.' The President, his facial expression inscrutable, looked at Shashlik before adding: 'It was a terrible loss.'

The young Minister, unsure whether the President's last comment was a reference to the demise of the Professor or to the fate that had befallen the noble vintage, nodded sympathetically. The President continued:

'When the news was relayed to me, I arranged for a team of our own officials to be flown out immediately to conduct a full investigation and, of course, perform an autopsy. A detailed examination of the Professor's body revealed that the unfortunate man had suffered a massive heart attack. Arrangements were made immediately for the Professor's remains to be brought back to the land of his birth for cremation.'

The President, unblinking, looked in turn at each of his Ministers.

'Naturally, the Professor's death affected us all deeply. As Head of State it was my duty to personally compose the obituary which appeared the following day in *Pravestia*. I believe that what I wrote was most apposite. I quote from memory: "The professor's tragic demise was as much a loss to popular music as it was to Physics. His passing leaves a much-needed gap." '

As he recounted these traumatic events, the President's anger had abated. He looked at Shashlik and smiled.

'Nevertheless, young man, your idea is not without merit. In the absence of anything remotely sensible from our other colleagues,' he stared contemptuously at the rest of the Cabinet, 'I shall look forward to hearing your proposal in much greater detail.'

'Certainly, Mr. President, I shall be honoured,' responded Shashlik eagerly. 'I shall make sure that all relevant information is on your desk by nine o'clock tomorrow morning.'

'Very well,' said President Sonofábic. 'We shall discuss your plan over breakfast tomorrow in my private office. I shall expect you at six o'clock – sharp!'

The President rose and, pointedly ignoring his subordinates, strode briskly from the room.

Eleven

The freshly-ground Colombian coffee – supplies of which were received by the President on a regular basis, along with other even more stimulating products from that region of South America – bubbled gently in his new electric percolator. The croissants, baked several hours earlier in Paris and flown in by special courier, were still warm and mouth-wateringly flaky. The Minister for Arts and Popular Culture had had no idea that his leader possessed such epicurean tastes.

The President rang a small, silver bell. Silently, a servant appeared and cleared away the Wedgwood crockery. Shashlik was impressed but judged that it would be wise not to enquire about the provenance of such luxury items. The President glanced at his Cartier watch.

'Now, young man, let us get down to business. Time is pressing. Tell me exactly how you propose to put your plan into practice.'

'Mr. President,' began Shashlik, 'there are many valuable lessons to be learnt from the disaster of our previous attempt to win the Eurovision Song Contest. Firstly, it is abundantly clear that the Professor – and please believe me, I would not dream of speaking ill of the dead, so I say this with the highest respect – the Professor was an incompetent amateur who possessed not the slightest knowledge or understanding of contemporary popular music.'

The President nodded in agreement and gestured to the younger man to continue.

'In order for the plan that I am about to put before you to succeed, it is essential that we obtain the services of a first-rate professional songwriter, a person who has a proven reputation in the popular music industry, someone who can be depended upon to create what in the West they call *hits*. Such a person will be the catalyst for bringing prosperity to Slavonicia and of course, Mr. President,' Shashlik smiled slyly, 'for assuring the continuation in power of the present government for many years to come.'

The President nodded enthusiastically. He mused aloud.

'So we require a man who can create *hits* – a *hitman*!' He laughed loudly at his little joke as private memories of the unfortunate Professor's fate were resurrected. 'The term is most appropriate!'

Shashlik laughed dutifully along with his leader, without really understanding why. The President's mirth finally subsided.

'Do you have any particular person in mind for this exceptional task? Your name is Mikael, is it not? I shall call you Mikael.'

'Yes, Mr. President. Thank you. I have indeed identified a person who, I believe, would satisfy perfectly our requirements for this project. I suggest that we dispatch as soon as possible a special envoy charged with the task of recruiting him. Having done this, he would then arrange for him to come to Slavonicia. Once here, his mission would be to find and rehearse a singer or a band which would perform the Eurovision-winning song that he would compose.'

Shashlik paused for a moment; he did not wish to appear too presumptuous. 'That is, of course, Mr. President,' he added hastily, 'if you are in agreement.'

The President smiled. 'I am impressed by your enthusiasm, Mikael. You will go far. But do not allow yourself to be carried away! Tell me; this musical genius, this potential saviour of Slavonicia, does he have a name?'

'Yes, please forgive me, Mr. President; he is an Englishman, a songwriter who is at the very summit of his profession. The list of his successes is most impressive. It was his creative genius that made a pretty young Australian girl called Kylie Minogue, an actress in a popular television programme in her native land, into a world-famous singer. The name of this outstanding individual, Mr President, is Peter Waterman.'

The President's features gave no indication that the name was familiar to him. His musical tastes were somewhat more conservative.

'You are remarkably well informed, Mikael; your intelligence network does you great credit.'

'Thank you, Mr. President,' replied the younger man. Shashlik felt that it would not be a good career move to divulge that the source of his information was, in fact, his ten-year-old daughter who spent most of her free time listening to American and British pop music on the miniature multi-band radio that he had brought back as a present from one of his fact-finding trips abroad.

Encouraged by his leader's positive response, Shashlik pressed on.

'This man would undoubtedly be able to meet our requirements – especially if we were able to make him a proposition which was financially attractive.'

'Ah!' sighed the President, 'there is always a price to pay. And money, as you are no doubt well aware, is currently something of a problem given the, shall we say, delicate state of our nation's economy.'

Shashlik nodded and smiled. 'Mr. President, I believe that I have a solution to this aspect of the plan. If you are in agreement, I would recommend that small, select units of our military be seconded from their normal duties to carry out a series of what it might be appropriate to describe as capital release operations, involving the reallocation of the necessary funds from provincial banks in neighbouring countries. As such events are nowadays, most regrettably, extremely commonplace, they would attract hardly any attention from the media. By means of such, er, involuntary transfers of assets, considerable sums of cash could be raised very rapidly and with minimal effort. There would be no need for violence – unless, of course, it proved absolutely unavoidable – and we would soon possess sufficient funds to pay Mr. Waterman's consultancy fees.'

The President was now beaming broadly.

'I congratulate you, Mikael. Your logic is impeccable.' He leant back in his high-backed leather chair and swivelled to face the bullet-proof window.

'Every time that there is a crime or an accident in one of these Western countries,' he mused, 'it is the bloated insurance companies who pay. The means of raising money that you have proposed will not fly in the face of the profound and inviolable principles of socialism that form the bed-rock of our glorious nation.'

He swung round to face the younger man and smiled.

'You have my authority to proceed, and with all haste. With regard to your suggestion about the operatives who would carry out these missions, I shall inform the Secretary for Defence that I am putting you in charge of a special, top-secret project which will have far-reaching consequences for the future of our country. Ever since his involvement in the Albanian air-to-sea missiles fiasco, he has been indebted to me for not being dismissed from his post. He will know better than to ask any awkward questions.'

The President rose from his seat, came round to the other side of the desk and embraced Shashlik in a bear-hug.

'I wish you good fortune, Mikael; the fate of Slavonicia lies in your hands.'

Twelve

There was nothing to suggest that the gathering in London of the European Heads of State was anything other than a routine get-together of political allies. The sole item of business on the official agenda was to discuss the increasingly pressing issue of global warming.

It was the custom for the chairman of such conferences to be the Head of Government of the host country. In exceptional circumstances, the Deputy Prime Minister was entrusted with the task; on this occasion, however, neither was available.

At the suggestion of Sir Douglas Anstruther, the Deputy PM had been dispatched to the Middle East for a five-day international symposium on world poverty being held at the twelve-star Dubai Intergalactic Hotel. As Sir Douglas had told his leader, the global warming issue was far too important and delicate a matter to be entrusted to a man whose diplomatic skills and command of English possessed all the subtlety of an elephant reversing into a greenhouse. The PM had been only too happy to agree to the Scot's suggestion that he, Sir Douglas, be charged with chairing the London meeting.

As he had explained at the start of the session, the PM was unable to attend for reasons that, he was sure that his distinguished colleagues would understand, were highly confidential. In a personally signed note to each of his fellow Heads of State, the PM had offered his most sincere apologies. However, he expressed his absolute confidence that Sir Douglas would prove to be a more than adequate substitute. He would go so far as to say that anything proposed by his most valued and trusted colleague would have his full backing.

The discussion followed predictably familiar lines. The representative of each country present deplored the rapidly growing threat to the world environment caused by industrial pollution but, with the deepest regret, maintained that it would not be possible to commit to reducing the production of toxic waste below their present levels.

One after another, each of the politicians pleaded that the already fragile economy of their own country would be irreparably damaged by such a reduction, that hundreds of thousands of jobs would be lost, that there would be a ruinous reduction in taxation revenue, and so on, and so on. The only product of this meeting was, appropriately, the copious emission of hot air.

Sir Douglas's patience was wearing thin; having had enough of all this blether he called the meeting to order.

'I am sure we all appreciate, ladies and gentlemen, that the issue of global warming is of paramount importance for the future of our respective countries and, indeed, for that of the entire world. However,' - he spoke slowly, establishing brief eye contact in turn with each of the people seated around the mahogany oval table - 'in recent days a rather more pressing matter has arisen; it is one which, if we choose to ignore it, could well render irrelevant the discussions in which we have been engaged this morning.'

His words - spoken in the deep Fifeshire tones that had changed not a jot during the more than four decades that he had spent south of the border - aroused the curiosity of his audience. Sir Douglas had a reputation for being a man who chose his words with great care and who did not exaggerate; he had their full attention.

*

The Prime Minister's endorsement of his colleague, although sincere, did not do him full justice; there were few, if any, more accomplished men in the world of international diplomacy than Sir Douglas Anstruther.

The Scot's career had progressed seamlessly from school to Oxford and thence to the Foreign Office. For over forty years, since joining in 1956, in the months following the Suez fiasco, he had served with quiet distinction a succession of political masters, the most recent of whom had authorised him to attend Cabinet meetings as his unofficial 'eyes and ears'. The PM recognised that Sir Douglas was far too valuable to be shackled to some tediously restrictive ministerial brief.

*

Douglas Anstruther was the son of a sheep farmer near the village of Strathmiglo, north of Edinburgh. He had never known his mother, who had died giving birth to him, her only child. There being few distractions on the farm, and even fewer children of his age in the locality, the young boy, whose father had never remarried, had experienced a largely solitary childhood.

As he grew up Douglas developed a voracious appetite for reading; he never lacked for company as he devoured omnibus editions of the adventures of the Scarlet Pimpernel and Sherlock Holmes, given to him by one of his teachers at the primary school he attended in a neighbouring village. When his father returned from his occasional visits to Edinburgh, he would bring back, as a special treat for his son, the latest issue of the Rover, Wizard and Adventure. The derring-do of British secret agents constantly outfoxing the Nazi swine enthralled the young boy. Who needed friends, he thought, when one had companions such as these?

At the age of ten Douglas won a scholarship to Edinburgh Academy; from his very first day, his appetite for learning marked him out as someone who would go far. His teachers referred to him affectionately as "two brains Anstruther" and, as he was very modest about his abilities, he enjoyed great popularity with his peers, also. None of them was surprised when, at the precocious age of sixteen, he won an open scholarship to St. Judas's College, Oxford, to read Mathematics.

Within a few weeks of arriving at The Double Cross, as the college was facetiously referred to in Oxford academic circles, Douglas found that his studies in numerical analysis, which often had his fellow-students scratching their heads, made insufficient demands on his intellect. Not one to savour the joys of idleness, he was constantly looking for fresh challenges.

Fascinated by the infinite possibilities of mathematics, he amused himself by devising and developing a number of brain-teasing puzzles. One, in particular, engrossed his attention. Requiring logical reasoning rather than mathematical expertise, the puzzle consisted of rows and columns, divided into a number of segments, each of which had to contain the numbers one to nine. After a time, he grew tired of the idea and turned his attention from numbers to words. The *Times* crossword irritated him, not because it was too difficult but because it took him, on average, only four minutes to complete.

Late one Thursday afternoon during his second year as an undergraduate, Douglas completed an essay on Calculation and Coincidence for the following day's tutorial. He looked at his watch; yes, he thought, there was just enough time for him to do what he had in mind before the evening postal collection.

He spent the next hour compiling a more challenging crossword puzzle than the one that had taken him three and a half minutes to solve that morning and sent it in to the *Times*. He received, by return, an invitation to take over as the regular setter of the notoriously fiendish Thursday crossword, whose previous compiler had recently been diagnosed with a terminal illness. Perhaps, wondered the young man, it was for that reason that the puzzles had seemed to be getting easier recently.

When his fellow students found out about Douglas's latest achievement, his nickname, which had followed him to Oxford thanks to one of his fellow-pupils at the Academy, was immediately subjected to fifty per cent inflation; "three brains" Anstruther became the talk of Oxford.

*

Having already mastered French and Latin at school Douglas decided in his last year at St Judas's to occupy some of his spare time by teaching himself Italian. As Finals week approached Douglas, more from boredom than stress, decided to practise his Italian language skills by translating into English his favourite bedside book, Machiavelli's *Il Principe.* Douglas was particularly intrigued by the political philosopher's thesis that the ends justified the means. The task of producing a faultlessly idiomatic version of *The Prince* in English took Douglas less than a week.

There was a further motive for his excursion into this new language; Magdalena, a pretty but shy girl who worked as a waitress in her parents' coffee bar in the High, had taken his fancy. The young Scot discovered, however, that his failure to make any headway was due to his inability to speak her language which he had mistakenly assumed to be Italian. A framed print on the wall behind the counter provided the clue that she came from a small village called Penuria in northern Sicily and that her silence was due to the fact that, having led a very sheltered life, she spoke only her local dialect. Her command of English was virtually non-existent.

The young would-be suitor realised that a considerable challenge lay before him if he was to establish a relationship with the young woman. There was only one way in which he could achieve his objective.

Over the following week he devised a dozen exceptionally fiendish cryptic crosswords for the *Times* and sent them in to the editor, confident that they would keep the newspaper's readers occupied each Thursday over the ensuing three months; Douglas had made his own plans for the long vacation before returning to Oxford to take up the research fellowship that he had been offered.

Thirteen

The overnight ferry from Naples docked just as the sun was coming up over Palermo. Douglas came down the gangway with a rucksack on his back containing a sleeping bag and a plastic ground sheet as well as his passport and money. He was pushing a second-hand bike, bought the previous day after he had arrived by train in the southern Italian city. Through the early morning mist, he could just make out the slopes of Mount Etna which, he had read, was liable to erupt without warning. From what he had heard about the people of Sicily, he hoped that they would turn out to be rather less volcanic.

After briefly consulting a map of the island to confirm his destination, the young man set off. He had calculated that it would take him several hours to reach it, even if he avoided getting a puncture on the rough country roads. He looked up, shielding his eyes against the sun. It was going to be a very hot day; he decided that it would be best to try to cover as much of the distance as possible before the temperature became unbearable.

Within a few minutes he had left the port area behind and was soon cycling along a deserted road that was little more than an unmade track. An hour or so later the sun had burnt off the early morning haze and the air was clear beneath a cloudless sky. Douglas breathed in deeply; this was real freedom! He hoped that he would soon have the opportunity to encounter some of the local people and start to pick up a little of the dialect that would help him in his self-imposed mission.

Without warning, two young men emerged from behind a tree by the roadside and planted themselves directly in front of him. Each of them had a handkerchief masking his face. The taller one pointed an ancient-looking shotgun at Douglas's chest. His companion started to shout and gesticulate. Although the student could not understand the specific words, their sense was abundantly clear; he had no choice but to hand over his rucksack. They motioned to him to lie face down in the dusty road.

The shorter Sicilian pointed at Douglas's bike and asked his friend a question. He responded with a laugh and, for good measure, spat on the ground. A moment later they departed as rapidly as they had arrived.

Douglas, somewhat shaken by the experience, picked himself up, brushed the dust off his clothes and continued on his way, not sure where to go but hoping to find a policeman to whom he might report the incident.

A few minutes later a black saloon car sped past him. Going much too fast for the narrow winding road, it disappeared round a bend. Seconds later Douglas heard a squeal of brakes and the sound of rending metal. Disregarding his own recent misfortune, he pedalled furiously after the car.

The vehicle had hit a huge rock that had been left in the roadway probably, Douglas guessed, by the same villains who had held him up only a few minutes earlier. Through a thick cloud of smoke he could just make out the driver, a young man about the same age as himself. He was slumped over the steering wheel and showed no sign of movement. There was a strong smell of petrol. Douglas ran over to the car, opened the driver's door and managed to pull the unconscious occupant to safety. Seconds later there was a loud explosion and the vehicle was engulfed in flames.

Douglas knelt down beside the young man; apart from a nasty looking bruise on his forehead he did not appear to have suffered any serious injury. Douglas took a water flask from his saddlebag and held it to the victim's lips. His eyes flickered open and he mumbled a few words. To Douglas they sounded similar to the language that his two assailants had used a few minutes earlier.

Douglas asked him one or two questions in Italian. He learned that the name of the man whom he had rescued was Giuseppe and that he lived in a small village a few kilometres away. With a combination of Italian phrases and sign language, Douglas conveyed the suggestion that he could get Giuseppe back to his village if he were able to ride pillion on his bike. The young man smiled his acceptance. The cycle wobbled erratically along the road for the hour or so that it took them to reach their destination.

The following day Giuseppe had recovered almost completely from his close encounter with death and the two young men discovered that they were able to converse in Italian with remarkable ease. Giuseppe told him that he had recently graduated from the University of Florence and revealed that he also spoke English.

The young Sicilian was curious to know why Douglas had come to such a remote place. The Scot explained his desire to pick up enough of the local dialect to enable him to converse with a girl he had met back home in England. He told Giuseppe that she was from a place called Penuria.

'By the way, Giuseppe, is Penuria anywhere near here?' asked Douglas. Giuseppe roared with laughter but did not answer. Instead, he responded with a question of his own:

'Tell me, where is your home?' he enquired, still laughing.

Douglas told him that he had been brought up in Scotland but that he was studying at Oxford.

'But that is where my parents live, with my younger sister!' exclaimed Giuseppe. 'This is an amazing coincidence!'

'She wouldn't, by any chance, be called Magdalena, I suppose?' asked the young Scot, who did not believe in coincidences.

Giuseppe shook his head. He noted with interest the expression of dejection on his new friend's face. Suddenly, Giuseppe roared with laughter and slapped him on the back.

'Yes, my friend! My sister's name *is* indeed Magdalena. I was, how do you say, pulling your leg!'

*

As he and Douglas were sipping their after-dinner coffee, Giuseppe filled in the details. His parents had sold their farm at far less than its real value to a neighbouring landowner before leaving Sicily with Magdalena to seek a better life in England. They had heard that Italian coffee bars were becoming increasingly popular with young people. They reasoned that they would have the best chance of success in a town where there was a large student population. The only two places they had heard of, apart from London, where they felt there would be too much competition, were Oxford and Cambridge; the matter had been decided by the toss of a coin.

Giuseppe had chosen not to accompany his family to England, preferring to pursue his studies at University in Italy. Laughing, he confided to Douglas that he, too, was involved in an amorous quest; he had been courting the only child of the neighbouring landowners and was intending to marry her with a view to eventually repossessing what he considered to be rightfully his family's property. The girl was moderately attractive, too, he told Douglas, which made his mission less unappealing than it might have been.

Giuseppe invited Douglas to spend the rest of the summer with him.

'That would be ideal, Giuseppe, especially if I may ask you one favour.'

'Anything, my friend; just tell me what it is.'

'Will you teach me the local dialect? I really would like to be able to talk with your sister when I get back to Oxford.'

Giuseppe was more than happy to oblige.

*

Douglas's thoughts turned to how he was going to be able to return home without his passport.

'I really should report the matter to the police,' he said to Giuseppe. The young man smiled.

'I regret to have to tell you that the police in these parts are incompetent.'

Douglas's face fell.

'But do not worry, my friend; in Sicily we have our own ways of dealing with such matters. Do not trouble yourself; you may leave everything to me.'

The following evening, as they were finishing dinner, Giuseppe told his friend that he had a present for him. Douglas opened the large package. Inside, as well as his rucksack and passport, there was a thick bundle wrapped in newspaper.

'What's this?' he asked Giuseppe.

'Open it,' replied his friend with a smile, 'and you will see.' Inside was a wad of banknotes, a much greater sum than had been stolen by his attackers.

'I don't understand, Giuseppe,' said the Scot. 'How did you manage to find out who had robbed me?'

Giuseppe smiled and explained that he had simply made a few enquiries. It seemed that two youths from a neighbouring village had suddenly started to spend more money than usual in the local *taverna*. Giuseppe had asked one of his cousins, a blacksmith by trade, to have a word with them.

'My cousin Luigi knows everyone in the area and everything that goes on. He struck up a conversation with them and invited them to share with him a couple of bottles of our local wine. After a while he brought up the matter of their new-found wealth. The lads could not hold their liquor – I believe that is the expression? - and they soon provided all the information that we required. Luigi brought them to see me yesterday, after you had retired for the night.

'In such cases,' continued Giuseppe, 'the ends justify the means, as our own Machiavelli pointed out several centuries ago. I simply used simple reasoning to help them to fully appreciate their position.'

'What on earth did you say, Giuseppe?' asked Douglas, intrigued.

'I asked them if, perhaps in a few years' time, they might wish to marry and produce children. Naturally, they agreed that this was what they wanted above all. As I am sure you know, Douglas, the sense of family continuity is very well developed in Sicily,' smiled Giuseppe. 'I then asked them if they would like to continue to possess the means to achieve their ambition.'

Douglas looked blank for a second or two before his friend's meaning became clear.

'Surely, you didn't say that you would … '

Giuseppe smiled and said nothing.

*

By the end of September Douglas had achieved, thanks to Giuseppe, an impressive degree of fluency in the local dialect. He had enjoyed the summer months in Sicily but was now looking forward eagerly to returning to Oxford to pursue his courtship of Magdalena. As he was about to board the ferry, Giuseppe embraced him.

'Tell my parents and my sister that I miss them very much,' he said with tears in his eyes. Giuseppe gave Douglas a sealed envelope. 'Please give this to Magdalena.' His eyes twinkled. 'I wish you *buona fortuna* in your quest.' Giuseppe paused for a moment; his normally cheerful face had assumed a serious expression.

'Douglas,' he said, clasping his friend to him with both arms, 'I shall never forget that you saved my life. If there is ever anything I can do in return, anything at all ...'

Fourteen

All the representatives of the European countries present at the meeting were, in terms of political status, senior to Sir Douglas. The tall, thin, silver-haired Scot possessed, however, an aura which commanded instant respect. They looked at him, expectantly.

'Distinguished colleagues,' he began, 'I hope that you will forgive me for having brought us all together under false pretences to discuss the effect of greenhouse gases. It was necessary to create - how shall I put it - a smokescreen between ourselves and the outside world. It is a necessary cover for the real issue that we must now address as a matter of urgency. As we are all well aware, the current situation in Barakistan is extremely volatile. My government is reliably informed that the Barakistanis are developing, in what they regard as conditions of absolute secrecy, a nuclear energy programme. Whilst the Barakistanis insist that they are engaged on such research for purely peaceful purposes, I am sure we all agree that such a state of affairs poses potentially grave problems. Already, the world's stock markets are showing signs of nervousness. The military and economic implications for the nations that we have the honour to represent are obvious. Also, for a number of you, I believe, general elections are approaching.'

Sir Douglas looked in turn at each of the men and women seated around the table and allowed them a moment to digest his words. He continued:

'There is little doubt that the situation could become extremely dangerous if nothing is done to, er, adjust this situation.'

Around the table there were nods and murmurs of assent. How succinctly Sir Douglas had summed up the situation! But what could be done? All previous diplomatic efforts with the infuriating Barakistanis had been a waste of time; they seemed to take a sadistic delight in stalling over every tiny detail.

After a few moments the meeting settled down; once again, all eyes were on Sir Douglas.

'Ladies and gentlemen,' he continued urbanely, 'with your permission, I should like to suggest a possible solution to this dilemma.'

This time there were no interruptions. Sir Douglas continued:

'As all of us who live in the West are well aware, our own nuclear defensive capability, under the umbrella of NATO, has guaranteed peace in Europe and beyond since 1949.'

Sir Douglas paused to polish his spectacles before continuing.

'Barakistan, however, as we know only too well, is a rogue state and, what is more, is marginally out of range of our current generation of ballistic missiles. It is undoubtedly their knowledge of this fact that has led its government to believe that it cannot come under attack from our forces for the foreseeable future. This has encouraged the Barakistanis to press ahead on what could well prove to be a catastrophic course.'

Heads nodded judiciously.

'What we require,' continued Sir Douglas, 'is a military base which is within striking distance of Barakistan, but one which, at the same time, does not put any of our own territories at risk from nuclear attack from that quarter.'

As he paused momentarily to take a sip of Highland Spring mineral water, the silence was immediately filled by the simultaneous responses of several national leaders:

'Naturally, we should be totally in favour of such a proposal, but regret that we could not be seen to …'

'It would not be possible, unfortunately, to …'

'The presence of such a military base would be seen as provocative and consequently …'

Sir Douglas, like a teacher faced with an unruly class, rapped the table twice with his pen. The noise immediately subsided. His own voice, although remaining suave, now had a touch of asperity.

'Ladies and gentlemen, I am sure that we all share similar concerns. However, I believe that there may be a way in which we can, so to speak, square the circle. If I may crave your indulgence I shall attempt to illustrate.'

Sir Douglas walked over to the window and pulled down the blinds. Then he crossed over towards the wall on the opposite side of the room and pressed a button. Noiselessly, a large-scale colour relief map of Europe and Western Asia unfurled. He pointed at it with a long, bony finger.

Everyone at the table looked uncomprehendingly at the map, then at Sir Douglas, seeking enlightenment. Although his features remained impassive, he was enjoying the moment. Some of these people, he thought, really were second-rate; it was no wonder that we got ourselves into such messes. Perhaps it was now time to illuminate their intellectual darkness. He proceeded to develop his proposal.

'For such a base we should require a location which is flat, so that runways of sufficient length could be constructed to accommodate our force of long-range bombers. There must also be, of course, protection from the possibility of invasion by land or sea.'

'But such a place does not exist!' ventured one of the more impulsive members of the gathering.

Resisting the temptation to contradict him directly, Sir Douglas began to elaborate his plan.

'I believe that here, ladies and gentlemen, is the solution to our little difficulty.' He pointed to a small area on the map.

'There it is, ladies and gentlemen,' he said, managing to keep any note of triumphalism out of his voice, 'Slavonicia!'

The assembled politicians squinted to get a better view of this place of which none of them had ever heard. Sir Douglas waited for a moment before continuing.

'Slavonicia, as some of you may already be aware, is a remote, landlocked and mountainous country. Its shape rather resembles that of a tooth, a molar to be precise, with ridges around its edges and vast, flat plains in the interior. It is, furthermore, comfortably within missile range of Barakistan. There could be no more ideal location for our purposes.'

The babble broke out once more.

'Fantastic! Amazing!'

'But would the Slavonician government agree?'

'What possible benefit could there be for Slavonicia itself?'

Sir Douglas ignored the questions and pressed on.

'By a happy coincidence, I shall be dining with the President of Slavonicia this very evening – purely a social engagement, of course. The President is currently paying a private visit to this country; I understand that he is over here to see his daughter. The Prime Minister had been intending to invite the President to an informal dinner at Number Ten but, as I believe I mentioned earlier, he has suddenly found that, unfortunately, he will not be free. Consequently the PM has asked me to entertain the President on his behalf. He was kind enough to suggest that, as the President's daughter is at present an undergraduate at my old Oxford college, we might discover some subjects of mutual interest. Naturally, I said that I should be delighted to have the opportunity to do so and perhaps to talk, off the record of course, about one or two other matters. If you will permit me, ladies and gentlemen, I should be happy to explore informally with the President the plan that I have outlined and report back to you as soon as possible. Would that meet with your approval?'

This time, there were no dissenting voices.

*

The meeting ended with a rare display of unity. The press *communiqué*, prepared several weeks beforehand, was issued in time to make the lunchtime news bulletins and the early editions of the evening papers. It reported in typically bland terms that useful progress had been made concerning the issues of global warming and related matters. Nobody thought to query what these related matters might be.

Fifteen

The seven-storey Ministry for Arts and Popular Culture occupied an entire block on the recently renamed Progressiy Strat in the centre of Bograd, the capital of Slavonicia. The building, constructed of solid granite, in common with the majority of the capital's other public edifices, had been erected during the Moscow-controlled communist régime.

On the façade of the uppermost floor, facing the street some thirty metres below, statues of lions, gladiators and assorted pagan divinities, all sculpted in a lurid turquoise, projected outwards, as if defying anyone to attack and thereby risk being torn to shreds by their metallic teeth and tridents.

If the statuary had achieved the purpose intended by its architect of intimidating the citizens of Bograd, it had in no way inhibited the city's bird population. Over the years they had added a thick, off-whitish coat which, according to the local wags, was their silently eloquent comment on the successive governments under which the country had been ruled.

All but a handful of the three hundred and ninety-one rooms in the Ministry building stood empty. It was government policy, however, to keep the electric lights burning day and night in every one of them, despite the vast expense, to create the impression that important government work was continuing ceaselessly. Few people, however, were ever seen entering or leaving; any passing members of the public who ventured inside were able to penetrate no further than the reception desk, behind which a uniformed colossus, who appeared to have been constructed from the same material as the building itself, sat impassively, protecting his masters.

Beyond the desk was an imposing wooden door on which a brightly polished brass sign announced 'Secretariassy'. The secretariat was, in fact, no more than a cramped and sparsely furnished room which had a sole regular occupant; Tatiana, a well-endowed eighteen-year-old, chewing gum and diligently filing her nails, sat in front of a bulky computer monitor, gazing open-mouthed at the cartoon screen-saver.

It was evident to even the most casual observer that the young girl's qualifications for the post were more physical than intellectual. She had been cherry-picked, literally, by the former Education Minister, who had come across her while visiting a training college as part of his official duties. During the subsequent job interview, the Minister had expressed a desire to acquaint himself more extensively with Tatiana's talents.

When news of this filtered back to the President, the libidinous Minister was moved to a less demanding post as Assistant Deputy Sub-Minister for Provincial Affairs. The young girl's silence had been secured by her appointment to the newly-created position of Senior Secretary at the Ministry of Arts and Popular Culture.

Tatiana's duties in her new job were not onerous. Consequently she was able to spend hours at a time on the telephone with her boyfriend, indulging their mutual taste for aural sex. In one of the brief interludes when she was not engrossed in intimate conversation, the telephone rang shrilly. Tatiana gave a start. Tentatively, she picked up the receiver.

'Hello? This is the Ministry for Arts and Popular Culture. How may I ...'

Before she was able to complete her Pavlovian response, her ears were subjected to the sort of language with which she was familiar from her own unconventional telephone conversations. On this occasion, however, the tone was totally lacking in sensuality.

'You wretched girl!' roared a furious male voice. 'I have been trying to get through to your office for more than an hour! What the devil have you been up to down there?'

The young girl, panicking, recognised the voice of the Minister. Although Tatiana had been brought up to always tell the truth, she judged correctly that on this occasion it might not be the wisest thing to do. Showing remarkable presence of mind, she came up with a suitable response.

'There, er, must have been a fault on the line, Minister. But,' she added cheerily if somewhat gratuitously, 'it seems to have cleared up.'

'Yes, well never mind about that now. I need you to do something urgently. Do you have a pen? Paper? Good. Write down this name!'

The phone line was indeed rather crackly. The nervous girl scribbled down on a scrap of paper what she thought she had heard. She did not dare to risk incurring the further wrath of her boss by asking him to repeat it.

'Have you got that?' said the Minister. 'Good. Now listen very carefully. I want you to locate this man. This - what is it called? - Internet can be quite useful, so I am told. The person you are to find is a musician, a song writer, in England. Yes, that is what I said, England. Yes, yes,' he said impatiently, 'where the Beatles came from. Yes, I'm sure that you are correct; yes, yes, Paul McCartney's songs are indeed very beautiful. Now stop interrupting, girl, and pay attention!'

The Minister spoke for a few more moments. Tatiana scribbled feverishly, trying to make sense of the torrent of information. 'Can you do that for me? Good girl.' Tatiana was relieved that he seemed to have calmed down.

'Let me have all the information you can find out,' he continued. 'I need full details about this person as soon as possible: the work that he does, where he lives, everything. This is a matter of national importance. Therefore, for reasons of State security, you must not – I repeat not – discuss this matter with anyone. With anyone at all, do you understand?' The Minister did not wait for a reply. The line went dead.

Tatiana, flustered by the brusqueness of the Minister's tone, hardly knew where to begin. Her virtual monopoly of the telephone for recreational purposes had left her little time in which to develop her computer skills. After several abortive attempts, Tatiana managed to penetrate the mysteries of the Internet.

Having overcome one difficulty, however, she was now faced with another; handwriting was not the most impressive of her educational attainments and she found it impossible to read what she had scribbled on the pad of paper. The first two attempts at keying in the name she thought she had written down proved unsuccessful. For a third time she squinted at the pad, trying desperately to decipher the two words. Her fingers jabbed erratically at the keyboard. Suddenly the screen went blank. 'My god!' she exclaimed, 'I have lost everything!'

Tatiana held her head in her hands and drummed her feet in frustration; she was sure that the Minister would be furious with her if she failed in what was clearly a crucially important task. She might even lose her job.

Her fears, however, proved groundless; a few moments later the monitor flickered into life. Tatiana sighed with relief. There could be no doubt about it; she had made an important breakthrough. She could see that what was now appearing on the screen in something called LIPA, appeared to match the two, barely legible words that she had written on her pad: Peter Wasserman.

Sixteen

The Liverpool Institute for Performing Arts had been set up only a few years previously by the former Beatles Paul McCartney and George Harrison. The old building, constructed in the early nineteenth century, had had a varied past. Originally used for the education of mechanics, it had eventually mutated into a High School for boys. Later still, after falling into disrepair, it had lain empty until the last decade of the twentieth century, when the two world-famous musicians had set about resurrecting the crumbling edifice.

Nowadays, LIPA specialised in dance, acting, sound technology – and music. The Institute's website gave full details of all its employees, from the Artistic Director right down to the humblest cleaner. Alongside the name of Peter Wasserman was his job: part-time assistant caretaker.

Tatiana could not understand it; why was this famous songwriter working in such a menial post? It didn't make sense. Then, suddenly, she understood the reason. Of course! Peter Wasserman's success in the music business over many years must have made him very wealthy. His occupation of such a lowly position was intended to make himself as inconspicuous as possible. Clearly, a man of his great talent had a *much* more important function. This job at LIPA was simply his *cover*! Perhaps he was really a *secret agent*! That would explain why the Minister had insisted that she must not breathe a word about this matter to anyone else!

Excitedly, Tatiana started to type up her report, her fingers struggling to keep pace with her fertile imagination, which had now gone into overdrive. Scenes from all those old James Bond films that she had watched so many times came rushing back. She pictured herself in the female lead role. It was so exciting! It was even better than the telephone conversations with her boyfriend. Her fingers trembled as, at the top of the sheet, she laboriously typed, in bold capital letters: TOP SECRET! HIGHLY CONFIDENTIAL! FOR EYES OF MINISTER ONLY!

*

For the young government official, the twenty-hour journey from Bograd had been a nightmare. There being no direct air connection between the capital of Slavonicia and the North West of England, he had had no choice but to endure several flights in a succession of cramped aircraft before arriving, hungry and exhausted, at Manchester Airport.

Petro Slivovic, in his early thirties, with short, fair hair, of medium height and athletic build, disembarked quickly from the plane, pushing his way past the assorted scruffy students and retired couples who had been his fellow sufferers on the budget-line aircraft.

Slivovic had been seconded from his post with the Slavonician Headquarters for Information and Tourism on the personal recommendation of its head. Wearing his habitual dark suit and plain tie, Slivovic had been chosen because of his unremarkable appearance and what his masters considered to be his fluency in English.

Once inside the terminal building, the young man extracted from an inside jacket pocket a single typewritten sheet. He consulted it one final time before carefully tearing the paper into tiny shreds.

Slivovic was travelling light, his only luggage a black leather briefcase inside which was a litre bottle of Grey Goose vodka purchased during the first stage of his journey from Bograd. There was nothing about his appearance to arouse the curiosity of even the most inquisitive Customs official as he negotiated passport control and walked briskly past the baggage reclaim area.

He was intent on getting away from the airport terminal as quickly as possible. The intelligence briefing that he had just been studying had referred to the notoriously acute shortage of taxis at English airports. Slivovic had made a mental note that his mission should not be delayed by his having to queue for a cab to take him to Liverpool. The first in the tortuous series of flights that was to take him back to Bograd was scheduled to take off from Manchester just before twelve o'clock that very night. He did not have a moment to lose.

*

'Where to, pal?' enquired the taxi driver.

'Begging pardon?'

'Where d'yer wanna go?'

'Lee-pa.'

'Yer what?'

'Lee-pa,' repeated Slivovic, reciting mechanically.

As the cabby still displayed no sign of comprehension, Slivovic expanded in a monotone on the mispronounced acronym.

'Lee-vair-pool Een-stee-toot off Pair-formin-Arse.'

'Oh, right! Gotcher, pal. I'll have you there in no time. Hop in.'

The taxi pulled away from the rank. Another cab moved slowly forward to fill the place it had vacated. Behind, a further twenty or so black hackney cabs each edged forwards a few metres.

As the taxi moved off, the driver was in a cheerful humour in anticipation of the hefty fare that he would be receiving. He could tell from the way Slivovic was dressed that he wasn't a tourist; he was probably a rich businessman, he thought, travelling on an expense account. The driver tried to strike up a conversation.

'Got important business at LIPA, 'ave yer?'

Slivovic froze in horror. How could this man have discovered the reason for his visit?! It was impossible! He was sure that he had left nothing to chance. Nevertheless, the young man knew that he had to be extremely careful; it was imperative that nothing went wrong. The best course of action, he decided, was to ignore the cabby's unsubtle attempt to extract top secret information from him. He reminded himself that he, Petro Slivovic, was a highly trained operative who had come first in his class at the Bograd Academy for Linguistic and Literary Studies. He permitted himself a silent snort of contempt; it would take much more skill than this clumsy amateur possessed to get anything out of *him*! He opened a copy of the previous day's *Pravestia*, thereby creating a flimsy but psychologically impenetrable barrier.

When the young man failed to reply, the driver gave up.

'Miserable bastard,' he muttered. 'Fuck 'im.'

Confident that his passenger had no idea of the distance between Manchester and Liverpool, the driver decided to exact revenge by taking a lengthy detour via Chester, thereby adding a considerable amount to the fare.

An hour and a half later, the taxi drew to a halt outside LIPA. Slivovic jumped out, opened his briefcase and thrust a handful of fifty pound notes into the cabby's hand.

'Is enough?' he asked.

The briefing document had omitted to provide Slivovic with information about currency exchange rates. Without waiting for a reply from the open-mouthed driver the envoy walked rapidly towards the entrance of the building.

'Fuck me!' exclaimed the cabby, looking in astonishment at the banknotes that his taciturn passenger had just given him.

Still in a state of shock at this windfall, the cab driver pulled away sharply from the kerb without indicating, narrowly avoiding collision with a car which was coming up behind him. Its furious driver sounded a long blast on his horn. The cabby responded digitally.

*

Slivovic elbowed his way through the tide of students who were flooding out of the Institute. As he made his way hurriedly into the building, concerned that the object of his quest might already have left, he failed to notice a middle-aged man with a pot belly walking in the opposite direction. This man, too, had his mind on the time - in his case, opening time at the pub. Having finished his shift, Pete Wasserman was now following his early evening ritual of getting a couple of pints down his neck before catching the bus back home to his bedsit in Toxteth.

More often than not, he got off the bus a couple of stops before the one nearest to where he lived. He didn't see the point of cooking a meal just for himself, especially as there was a decent chippy not far from where he lived where they did a good cod, chips and mushy peas.

Most evenings Doreen, a girlfriend from his teenage years before he had met Tina, was serving behind the counter. If her boss wasn't looking, she would slip a jumbo sausage into the greaseproof paper wrapping, with a smile and a wink, before concealing it under a mound of chips. She knew that Pete had been going through a bad time since his wife had left him. She had made several attempts to let him see that she was interested in him but Pete hadn't taken the hint.

If it wasn't raining, Pete would eat his supper as he slowly walked back home. He had lived there on his own since Tina had walked out on him and gone to live in Huyton with one of her younger sisters, who had never married.

As Pete walked along, his thoughts turned to Tina; he was really missing her. He knew that it was his own fault that she had left him and felt that there was nothing he could do to put matters right. It was too late now to try and make amends.

Seventeen

'You'll find Pete in the Navvy, pal,' said the doorman at LIPA, in answer to Slivovic's question.

'If you are pleasing, what is Navvy?' enquired Slivovic, whose command of English did not extend to colloquial abbreviations.

'The Navigation Inn, mate, it's a pub.'

The doorman, realising that he was talking to a foreigner, expanded on his explanation. He enunciated carefully, as if talking to a small and particularly obtuse child.

'It's a pub-lic house, where - you - go - for - a - drink' – he mimed raising a glass to his lips - 'with yer mates, like. Everyone round here calls it the Navvy.'

'I am thanking you muchly. Please to tell me, where it is being situate?'

The doorman's subsequent directions, although fairly straightforward, taxed Slivovic's comprehension of Scouse pronunciation beyond its limits. However, not wanting to give the impression that he had not understood, the envoy strode off purposefully; time was of the essence.

'Hoy! Mate!'

Slivovic turned round; the doorman was gesticulating to him.

'Yer goin' the wrong bleedin' way!'

Slivovic, cursing silently, turned round and set off on the correct course for the Navigation.

'Thick bugger!' muttered the doorman, as he went back inside the building.

A few minutes later Slivovic found the pub and pushed open the heavy swing doors. They reminded him of the Wild West saloons he had seen in old cowboy films on the single Slavonician television channel that was operational, when electricity supplies permitted, for as much as four hours each day. As he entered the public bar, he wrinkled his nose in disgust; the place stank of stale beer and cigarette smoke.

Slivovic went up to the bar behind which a large, tattooed Irishman was wiping his hands on a grubby towel. In this part of the city, being large, tattooed and Irish was virtually the job description for a publican.

'What'll it be, pal?' asked the barman. Slivovic managed to convey to him that he wanted not a drink but information:

'Peter Wasserman drinking here is at this moment in time?'

The barman, accustomed to dealing with customers whose powers of speech were temporarily impaired, had little difficulty in understanding Slivovic.

'He was sitting just over there,' he said, pointing to a vacant table in a corner of the room. 'You've just missed him. He'll be on his way home now, on the bus.'

Slivovic swore under his breath.

'Where is it that he living, barkeep?'

The ancient TV westerns had made a significant, if somewhat outdated contribution to his vocabulary.

'Dunno, exactly,' replied the barman, 'but he always gets the bus from just down the road.' He pointed in the direction of the bus stop.

Slivovic thanked him and hurried out of the pub.

He reached the bus stop just as the double-decker was moving off. Through a window he saw sitting downstairs a man he thought might be Pete. Slivovic looked round in desperation. As the bus disappeared into the distance he started to panic. The whole mission was in jeopardy! He must not lose his target now, after coming all this way.

Suddenly a black cab came into view. Frantically waving his arms Slivovic stepped into the road. The taxi stopped, its brakes squealing.

'Are yer' tryin' to get yerself killed, yer fuckin' idiot?' shouted the cabby. 'You was nearly fuckin' strawberry jam!'

Ignoring the driver's language, Slivovic grabbed the door handle and jumped into the taxi. As he got in, he remembered the old cops and robbers movies he had seen during his youth. Now was his chance to utter the words that he could never have imagined himself using. Slamming the door behind him he instructed the driver: 'Follow that autobus!'

*

Pete was a creature of habit. He got off the bus at the stop near the chippy and went in, fumbling in his pocket in the hope of finding a couple of quid with which to buy his tea. Inside the taxi, Slivovic leaned forward and banged on the glass partition to attract the driver's attention.

'Stop here!'

Jumping out of the taxi he pressed another of his seemingly endless supply of fifty pound notes into the hand of the astonished cabby.

'D'yer want me to wait, sir?' he asked respectfully.

'No, is OK. I walk.'

The cab driver sped off, not wanting to linger in case his passenger realised that he had given him far too much money and asked for change.

A few moments later Pete came out of the shop, eating a chip from the steaming packet. Slivovic came up to him.

'You are Peter Wasserman, is this not true?'

'Yeh, that's me. Who're you?'

'Please, do not be alarming. I am coming here to ask you help with most important mission.'

'Oh, yeh? What mission's that, then? Yer mean like James Bond?'

'Not exact, but I am thinking you will be interesting to hear what I am having to say, Mr. Wasserman. Very interesting indeed. Perhaps we go to public house or tavern where I tell you more.'

*

As he sipped the pint of lager that Slivovic had put down on the table in a quiet corner of the pub, Pete looked at him carefully. Even Stevie Wonder could see that this guy was a headcase; on the other hand, he also looked as if he could handle himself in a fight. Pete decided that it would be best if he agreed with everything the man said in case he turned nasty.

'You are very famed in our country, Mr. Wasserman,' said the foreigner. 'The young people of Slavonicia, they are big fanatics of your composings.'

After the third pint, Pete was impressed with what he had heard; maybe this guy wasn't such a nutter after all. When Slivovic suggested that they discuss the purpose of his visit in greater detail at Pete's place, his earlier reservations evaporated.

Slivovic prided himself on his ability to assess a person's character within a very short space of time. Installed in a sagging armchair back at Pete's bedsit, he could see immediately that Pete, far from being stupid, was merely being cautious. He had heard that these English were clever, cunning even. The Slavonician envoy knew from the briefing paper prepared by Tatiana that Pete's apparently lowly function at LIPA was no more than a cover. There was no way that a man of Wasserman's calibre would be so unprofessional as to discuss his work in detail with a perfect stranger. The man from Bograd decided to probe a little further before presenting the distinguished songwriter with his proposition.

'Your work at the Institute is of big importance,' ventured Slivovic. 'Without your valued contributing, I am sure that the place would go – how do you say? - down the pipes.'

Pete, one of whose responsibilities was to unblock the lavatories when they overflowed, nodded in agreement. Encouraged by his success in teasing out this admission, Slivovic pressed on.

'I am realising, of course, that much of work what you do is, er, underground.'

Pete, whose duties also included checking the central heating boiler in the basement, nodded again as he took another long swig from a can of lager. He was impressed; this foreign geezer seemed to know quite a bit about him.

Slivovic, for his part, had observed that Pete was a man of few words. This, in his opinion, was a good sign; Pete Wasserman was clearly someone who could keep his mouth shut and who would not be in danger of – he racked his brain to unearth another of those English idioms – what was it? Ah, yes! – releasing the feline from the sack.

The younger man opened his briefcase, took out the bottle of vodka and scanned the room, looking for a suitable receptacle. Pete went into the kitchenette and returned with two chipped pottery mugs. Slivovic unscrewed the cap of the bottle and filled Pete's mug almost to the brim.

'What about you, then?' asked Pete, as the other man put down the bottle on a table. 'Aren't you havin' none?'

'No, thanking you,' replied Slivovic. 'I have bad belly after journey,' he lied. 'If I drink vodka now I get sheets.'

'Why d'yer need shee..' asked Pete. He stopped suddenly in mid-question. 'Oh, I gerrit!' he smiled.

*

Between frequent sips of vodka, Pete listened as Slivovic told him about how during his teenage years he had listened to American and, especially, English pop music. He was especially keen, he said, on the Beatles, the Stones and all the singers and groups from the sixties. He confided to Pete that he had listened to their records in secret, at night, on a small transistor radio.

'When I was young boy, it not permitted to listen to Western music. But I liking it because it helping me learn English,' he informed Pete. 'It best way to learn, better than books,' he added.

Slivovic's enthusiasm made him bolder. 'I know many songs,' he continued. 'I learn words. I showing you: Doo wah diddy, diddy, dum diddy doo,' he warbled. The young man looked at Pete, seeking approval. 'You want I sing more?' Without waiting for a reply the Slavonician envoy embarked on another song made famous several decades earlier: 'Um, um, um, um, um, um,' he inarticulated.

'Manfred Mann and Wayne Fontana songs are big hits in our country,' he informed Pete. 'I am still remembering the words.' He looked at Pete proudly. 'This is how I am learning speak English so good.'

Under the Soviet régime, he told Pete, everything that originated in the West had been banned, but now that the bad old days had gone for ever, the people of Slavonicia were ready to embrace a new generation of popular music. Slivovic was sure that he, Pete Wasserman, was the man who could bring back the musical creativity of which his fellow-countrymen and women had been deprived for so long. There was a lot of talent in Slavonicia, he informed Pete, pouring another slug of vodka into his mug.

'My boss at Ministry,' said Slivovic, 'he know all about you. He send me here to ask you big question. He need talentuous songwriter for composing song, and then teach someone in my country how to perform it.'

Pete listened with interest; from time to time he added the odd detail about his own, short-lived career as a pop singer, casually dropping the odd name into the conversation: a Paul here, a Mick there. It was just like being at the Griffin, except that now he was drinking vodka instead of lager.

Slivovic, normally a man who showed little emotion, was visibly impressed by these reminiscences. This Peter Wasserman, he concluded, obviously had influential connections in the musical world, yet remained remarkably modest about his achievements. Listening to him talk, one would have thought that he had been nothing more than a player in a tenth-rate group and a composer of a song that had ended up on the B-side of a long-forgotten pop record.

Pete was feeling relaxed. This Petro guy was all right. In fact, it seemed to him that that they had a lot in common. After half an hour, the bottle of Grey Goose was three-quarters empty.

Slivovic looked at his watch; it was getting late. He thought that he had better get down to completing the mission for which his masters had sent him such a long way.

Pete listened in silence and ever-increasing amazement to what Slivovic had to say.

'And so,' concluded the envoy, 'Mr. Wasserman – Pete – I am authorised by my superiors to be offering you, in return for your professional servicing, the sum of twenty thousand English pounds. Sterling.'

Pete's mouth fell open. Twenty thousand quid! He tried for a moment to work out how long it would take him to earn that much at LIPA. After a few seconds he gave up; mental arithmetic was not his strong point. He stared in disbelief at his visitor. '*How* much?' he exclaimed. 'You must be fuckin' jokin'!'

Slivovic was totally unprepared for such a reaction. It did not take him long, however, to realise that he had been guilty of a serious miscalculation. There could be no doubt that the great songwriter had been deeply insulted by this offer which, as his reaction clearly indicated, he regarded as derisory. The instructions that Slivovic had been given were unequivocal: on no account was he to return without having secured the services of Peter Wasserman.

Slivovic needed to think quickly; how could he retrieve the situation? The prospect of reporting that his mission had failed filled him with terror. During the previous régime his superior officer had been in charge of the State prison service. The joke in the Ministry was that the old man had been expelled from the Stastzpolizi, the notorious State Secret Police, for cruelty. Slivovic was not keen to discover whether the rumour had any substance.

'Pete,' he pleaded, 'please accepting my apologising. My behaviour was totally inpropriate. I was not desiring of insult to a man of your great famousness. Please believing me, I not intending any disrespecting.'

Slivovic paused, unsure about how to proceed. If he made another offer, would Pete reject that, too? The envoy knew that he could not afford to make any more mistakes. The fate of Slavonicia, as well as his own, depended on how Pete reacted to what he was about to say. He could feel rivulets of sweat coursing down his sides from his undeodorised armpits. It was then that he remembered that strange English phrase: what was it? Yes! "Money no objection."

'Pete - Mr. Wasserman – Sir,' he ventured. 'The figure I mentioning was, of course, only an advancement sum to assure us of acquisition of your servicing. What is the word I am searching? Yes, that is it: detainer. If the song that you composing win Eurovision Song Contest for Slavonicia, our grateful nation will rewarding you in sum of quart ... half million English pounds. Sterling.'

It was fortunate for Pete that he had just gulped down the last mouthful of vodka, to steady his nerves. If the potent spirit had still been in his mouth as Slivovic had made his offer, the consequences would have been unsightly – and probably flammable.

Pete couldn't believe what he was hearing. For several seconds he looked suspiciously into his glass. Had Slivovic put something funny in it? He sniffed it again. It seemed OK. Pete stared at his visitor to see if he was pulling his leg but Slivovic's expression was expectant, almost pleading. A good ten seconds elapsed while Pete's brain, struggling to combat the effects of the vodka, tried to take in the fantastic proposition. Finally, he stretched out a hand.

'OK, pal,' he slurred, 'yer gorra deal.'

*

Petro Slivovic was as good as his word. Carefully opening his briefcase, he extracted a thick brown envelope and handed it over.

'Herein, please to find twenty thousand English pounds. Sterling. You wish me counting, yes?'

He informed the incredulous Pete that the rest of the money would be paid into a bank account of his choice on satisfactory completion of the contract.

Slivovic extracted another envelope from the briefcase. 'In Slavonicia,' he informed Pete, 'we priding ourselves on our efficientness, but also on our considerateness. We understanding that a man in your position is having - what is your phrasing? – many loose endings to attach.'

He held out the envelope to Pete.

'We want to economise your time so we have buyed already your passaging to Slavonicia.' Slivovic gave Pete another, smaller, envelope. 'Take please your aeroplane ticketings for the voyage to Bograd. We expecting you in one week. The journeying is very long and many differing aeroplanes are needed for conveying peoples to Slavonicia. When you arriving at Bograd airport you will be meeted by our interpretator, Irena,' he continued. 'She learn speaking English with records and books. She speaking even more better that I does.'

Pete was stretched out on the sofa, his eyes closed. To the casual observer it would have seemed that he was fast asleep. Slivovic, however, was not fooled by appearances; it was clear to him that Pete was deep in thought, already working out his plans for getting Slavonicia onto the world musical stage. What a professional, thought the agent.

Slivovic looked at his watch; he would have to hurry if he was going to get back to Manchester in time to catch the plane for the first stage of his long, circuitous journey back to Bograd. He gave Pete a farewell smile.

'Goodbye, Mr. Wasserman – Pete,' he said softly. 'It was big pleasure to meeting you. Now I go.'

Pete, a big smile adorning his features, did not respond. Slivovic picked up his empty briefcase, quietly closed behind him the front door of the bedsit and set off in search of a taxi. Christmas was going to arrive early for another lucky cabby.

Eighteen

Before Pete had been anaesthetised by the Grey Goose, Slivovic had impressed on him the need for total secrecy. Their agreement, he had said, was to remain absolutely confidential: Pete must say nothing about it to anyone. So far as his employers were concerned, he was simply to tell them that he had had a sudden domestic crisis – Slivovic was sure that a man with his creative gifts would be able to invent some convincing reason - and that he would not be able to come in as usual to work his shift.

When Pete finally awoke at about noon the following day, he had at first only the haziest recollection of what had occurred the previous evening. Perhaps, he thought, it had all been a dream. The only clues to the contrary were the empty vodka bottle lying on the floor by the sofa and the two envelopes on the table. He looked suspiciously at them as if they might explode. Swallowing hard he picked up the larger of them and emptied the contents onto the table. Thick wads of £50 notes came tumbling out. Pete was almost entirely lost for words. As he touched the money, fearful that it would suddenly disappear, all he could manage was a breathless 'fuckin' hell!'

Little by little, more of the details of his conversation with Slivovic came back to him. He remembered that the first thing he had to do was to get in touch with the Institute.

The phone in Pete's bedsit was no use; it had been cut off ages ago. He would have to use the phone box on the corner, near the Spar shop – he just hoped it hadn't been vandalised. Pete searched in vain for some coins. He was penniless – apart from the twenty thousand quid that Slivovic had left for him. Pete tore off the wrapper around one of the bundles of fifties and stuffed a handful of notes into his trouser pocket.

In the kitchen Pete found an old Kwik Save carrier bag into which he crammed the rest of the money. He closed the door of his bedsit behind him and with a spring in his step set off, whistling a favourite tune from the old days.

*

With great suspicion the woman behind the counter in the Spar shop examined the fifty pound note Pete had given her before grudgingly counting out his change. She might have been friendlier if his purchases had extended beyond a Mars bar and a copy of the *Star*.

He pocketed the various notes and coins and crossed the road to the phone box. To Pete's surprise, it had escaped the attentions of the local scallies and he managed to get through with hardly any delay to the Human Resources manager at the Institute.

She was very sorry, she said, to hear that his grandmother was so ill and hoped that Pete would be able to return to work soon when she had ... There was a silence.

'Died?' asked Pete, trying to be helpful.

'No, no,' spluttered the embarrassed voice at the other end of the line, 'recovered, is what I was going to say.'

'Well, you know what it's like with old people,' said Pete, who was getting into the role and starting to enjoy himself. 'Sometimes they can look like they're gonna pop off any second, and then they gerra bit better and hang on for ages.'

'You can say that again,' said the personnel officer, relieved that Pete had not taken offence. 'I had an uncle once who...'

Pete, now that his first task had been accomplished, realised that he needed to cut the conversation short. There were still quite a few things that he had to do that day. He pinched his nostrils with two fingers and imitated the warning 'beep...beep... beep'.

'Sorry, there's them pips. I'm in a phone box and I 'aven't got no more money. Gorra go now. I'll be in touch.'

*

Pete remembered what Slivovic had said about the rest of the money being paid into a bank of his choice once the job had been completed. Pete had never had a bank account. His dad had always warned him off banks. In his opinion all they did was charge you for giving you the privilege of letting them borrow *your* money.

Pete recalled a joke he had heard in the pub, a couple of weeks earlier: 'Why do the Irish call their currency the *punt*?' an old man had asked the barman.

'Dunno, pal. But you're gonna tell me, right?'

The old man had taken a long swig of his pint of Guinness before chortling triumphantly: 'Because it rhymes with bank manager!'

*

All Pete had to do now was to find a bank where he could deposit the money given to him by Slivovic. The first one he came across was the Royal Bank of Wales, an imposing building in the city centre. Pete pushed open the heavy door and joined a long queue of customers who were waiting with varying degrees of impatience. A businessman, trying to look important, was fiddling with the lock on his briefcase. Every few seconds he looked in irritation at his watch, tutting each time. He reminded Pete of that John Cleese off the telly.

A young mother was keeping an eye on her son, a stocky, crop-haired lad who looked about twelve years old. His face reminded Pete of a potato. The boy was scribbling on a leaflet which advertised what the bank described as its highly competitive services. The woman smiled indulgently at the lad.

'He loves writin', does our Wayne,' she announced proudly to nobody in particular. 'I bet he'll end up writin' loads of books.'

'Next, please,' called out a cashier. As Pete approached the counter, she looked disapprovingly over her glasses at the unshaven middle-aged slob who stood before her. Thank goodness for the reinforced glass, she thought.

'Yes?' she asked, icily.

'I wanna give youse some money, like.'

'You mean you wish to open an account?' she asked, incredulously. Honestly, she told her friend later during her lunch break, the man looked as though he had come straight from a Salvation Army hostel; he looked more like the sort of person you would expect to be *robbing* a bank, rather than depositing money in one.

'And how much would you be wishing to deposit, *sir*?' she continued with barely concealed sarcasm. Pete lifted the Kwik Save bag onto the counter and turned it upside down. Bundles of banknotes cascaded onto the counter. The cashier's eyes widened.

'Will this be enough, d'yer reckon?' enquired Pete, innocently.

Nineteen

The farthest Pete had travelled in his life had been to Stockport for the recording session with the Stumblebums, over thirty years earlier. He had never needed a passport and, until the previous day, it had not occurred to him that he ever would. Now he needed one - and fast. When he enquired at the Post Office, he was told that the process would take up to four weeks.

'That's no f...' Pete checked himself. 'That's no good. I've just found out that me old granny hasn't got long and I've gorra go and see her before, yer know, before ...' Pete was getting quite good at this.

The clerk became instantly sympathetic.

'Well, sir, we do offer an express service. Of course, you will need to produce an official copy of your birth certificate, which could take a few days to obtain if you haven't already got one. Once we've received it we could process your application the same day. But it is' – he hesitated, assessing the scruffy individual on the other side of the counter – 'it is more expensive.'

'Don't worry about that, pal. Me gran's me only livin' relative. She lives in Slav... in Eastern Europe. That's where me family come from, like, a long time ago.'

'Well, sir, I don't think there should be any problem. You'll need to provide two photographs as well, of course – there's a booth just over there - and get them countersigned on the back by a person of professional status who knows you well, your doctor, for example. Or perhaps you know a Justice of the Peace?'

Over the years Pete had indeed made the acquaintance of a number of JPs. It might be better, he thought, to get his GP to countersign the photos.

'Yeh, no problem,' he informed the helpful clerk. 'So if I come back in a few days, when I've got me birth certificate, you'll be able to do it on the spot, yer know, process me thingy?'

'Certainly, sir. That should be no problem at all.'

Pete thanked the man and walked out of the Post Office, humming.

*

Every day the tabloids were full of photos of pop stars, actors and other celebrities. Pete was surprised by how cool they always managed to look, even if they were wearing just a pair of jeans and a teeshirt. He was particularly impressed by McCartney, Pete's somewhat more successful contemporary. Noting the former Beatle's scruffily smart designer jeans and white, open-necked shirt, Pete reckoned that Paul would have no trouble finding someone to need and feed *him* in a few years' time, when he was sixty-four.

Pete's newly acquired wealth had boosted his confidence; if he was going to be a Eurovision-winning songwriter, he realised that he had better look the part; his current wardrobe simply would not do.

His physical appearance was another problem. A living testament to the long-term nutritional benefits of fast food and alcohol, Pete had to admit, when he looked in his bathroom mirror at the non-designer stubble and sagging jowls, that he was a wreck. Tina had nagged him constantly, too, about his beer belly but he had just ignored her. He had always reckoned that that was the secret when it came to handling women; the easiest way to avoid arguments was to agree with everything they said. And then carry on exactly as before.

In the old days, it had been Tina who had bought all Pete's clothes for him, right down to his socks and underwear. He hadn't minded that at all – he couldn't stand shopping anyway. The thought of all the queues and trying things on and standing in front of mirrors while other shoppers walked past, looking at you, made him shudder. Since Tina had left him, he had made do with second-hand clothes from charity shops. But now that he had plenty of money, he could buy whatever he wanted. Traipsing round the shops would be a pain but it was all, he convinced himself, in a good cause.

*

Seven days after his visit from Slivovic, Pete, kitted out courtesy of M and S and British Home Stores, locked the front door of his bedsit and, clutching his passport in one hand, rolled his new suitcase with the other as far as the corner of the street. He had thought briefly about getting the train to Manchester Airport but now that he was flush he thought 'fuck it', and decided to go all the way by taxi. He had never been in a cab before.

By one of those coincidences that usually happen only in fiction, the cabby turned out to be the same man who had brought Slivovic to Liverpool. The driver was pleased to find that this time his passenger was quite chatty. It was obvious, also, from the way he was dressed that he wasn't short of a bob or two.

When they arrived at the airport the cabby, anticipating a generous tip, put Pete's case down on the pavement and smiled at him.

'That'll be fifty quid exactly, mate.'

Pete put his hand in his trouser pockets, pulled out two twenties and a tenner, and held them out to the cabby.

'Here y'are, pal.'

The driver looked at the banknotes and then at Pete, who was already walking off, trailing his suitcase behind him.

'Tight bastard,' muttered the cabby, slamming the door as he angrily contemplated the drive back to Liverpool without a return fare.

Twenty

As the pilot released the brakes, the Boeing 737 shot down the runway like a stone from a catapult. Pete's stomach felt as if it was about a yard behind him. His hands gripped the armrests of his seat. Sweat broke from every pore. He screwed his eyes shut and waited for death.

A few seconds later there was a whirring noise followed by a 'whoomp - whoomp' sound. Not realising that this was the sound of the undercarriage being retracted, Pete could not understand why he wasn't feeling any pain. Was it a dream, he wondered, or was he already dead?

His terror was interrupted by a gentle tap on his arm. Pete opened his eyes and looked up to see a pretty young flight attendant standing over him. She was looking anxious.

'Are you all right, sir? Is there anything I can do for you? Perhaps you would like a glass of water? Or maybe you would prefer something a little stronger?'

The flight attendant's English was perfect, with only the slightest foreign inflection. Pete, breathing rapidly, struggled to reply. The smartly-dressed businessman sitting next to him smiled condescendingly.

'First time in one of these things, is it? Nothing at all to worry about when you fly Air Chance – sorry, Air France; just my little joke! These crates are as safe as houses, take it from me. It's all quite boring, really, this flying business. The only interesting part is wondering whether you're going to clear the perimeter fence. After that, it's all plain sailing – so to speak. And if, heaven forbid, the pilot doesn't make it, at least you'll not have to worry about it, ever again! Always look on the bright side, eh?'

If the man's intention had been to reassure his travelling companion, he had made a spectacular miscalculation. Rivulets of sweat ran down Pete's face, which changed from grey to green as his stomach reacted to the stress. He reached frantically for the paper bag in the seat pocket in front of him. He was a fraction of a second too late.

Apart from the malodorous damage caused to his fellow passenger's trousers and shoes, the rest of the flight to Charles de Gaulle airport passed without further incident.

*

After knocking back a couple of medicinal brandies before embarking on the next stage of his journey, Pete felt much better. He discovered in his jacket pocket the copy of the *Star* that he had bought at the Spar shop the previous day. In all the excitement he had completely forgotten to look at it.

He glanced at an article on page one – it seemed to be about some American couple called Fannie and Freddie who were having money troubles - before turning to the sports headlines. After twenty games City's expensive new number nine still hadn't managed to put the ball in the net. There was a quote from his manager who said he had total confidence in him and pleaded with the fans to be patient. The lad, the manager insisted, was a proven goal-getter; he would soon rediscover his scoring touch and be banging them in all over the place. City's chairman was quoted as having given his unqualified support to the unfortunate striker and his beleaguered manager.

As Pete was finishing the article about the footballer, the flight attendant came round with drinks and snacks.

'Is there anything else I can get for you, sir?' she beamed at Pete. She didn't speak like the other one, Pete noted; she sounded a bit more like Slivovic.

'Y'aven't got any of today's English papers, 'ave yer, luv?' he enquired.

The young woman smiled and delved into the recesses of her trolley. She emerged with the latest editions of the *Financial Times* and the *Star.* Pete opted for the tabloid. Ignoring the front page banner headline, he turned the paper over to discover that City's manager had been sacked and that the non-striking striker had been transfer-listed. The Club chairman, it seemed, was unavailable for comment; all calls to his mansion in the Isle of Man had gone unanswered.

Flicking through the rest of the paper, Pete discovered that Freddie and Fannie seemed to be doing much better. He envied them; he wished that he and Tina could have got back together just as quickly.

Pete flicked through the newspaper to see if there was anything else of interest. A brief article at the bottom of page seven caught his eye. According to news agency reports, a mysterious spate of small bank robberies had occurred during the past few days in several Eastern European countries. All the raids, it was reported, had had an identical *modus operandi*: in each case, two motorbike riders, dressed from head to toe in black leather, had held up a small, suburban branch of a major European bank. The number plates of the bikes had been removed. In total, the equivalent of just over half a million pounds had been stolen. The raids, apparently, had been carried out with military precision and no-one had been injured. The police, the article concluded, had no leads to go on.

Pete smiled to himself; just so long as they've not stolen *my* half million, he thought. Stuffing the newspaper into the magazine pocket of the seat in front of him, he settled down contentedly to doze for the remainder of the flight.

Twenty-one

The approach to Bograd airport is notorious among the world's civil airline pilots as one of the most difficult and dangerous challenges to their aeronautical skills. There are few days in the year when the runway is not shrouded in mist or low-level cloud. Consequently, both take-off and landing require nerves of steel and the capacity for split-second reaction to the unpredictable cross-winds coming in from the mountain peaks which rear up less than ten seconds' flying time from the end of the single, narrow strip of concrete.

Not surprisingly, all of the world's major airlines give Bograd the widest of berths, depositing would-be visitors to Slavonicia in the relative safety of Prague, Budapest or Belgrade. From there, passengers are left to undertake the final stages of their journey to the Slavonician capital in the care of smaller, more intrepid operators.

*

The distance between the plane and the terminal building at Bograd airport, a single-storey shed with a corrugated iron roof, was no more than fifty metres. The driver of the shuttle bus contrived to take five minutes to ferry the passengers to the drab structure from the small turbo-prop aircraft that had brought them from Belgrade. By the time the passengers had submitted themselves to a detailed check of their passports and managed to decipher the instructions on how to get to baggage reclaim, the motley collection of suitcases, holdalls and badly dented packages bearing large 'fragile' stickers had already done several circuits of the creaking baggage carousel.

As Pete was hoisting his bag off the conveyor belt, a strikingly beautiful young woman with long black hair came up to him. Her smile revealed perfect, white teeth.

'You are Mr. Pete Wasserman, yes? My name is Irena. I am representation of Slavonicia Ministry for Arts and Popular Culture.' She pronounced the word *cool-toor*. 'I am pronouncing rightly, yes? No?'

'Yeh, that's right, luv,' he replied. To Pete, the way she said it sounded just great.

'That is good, thank you. I am going to be your personal assistant and interpretator.'

She treated him to another dazzling dental display.

'I shall be delicious to reveal you the hidden wonderfulnesses of my beautiful koontree and putting your tongue into mine whenever you have need. I look forward very much to being attached to you. My little sister Tatiana is working at Ministry. She has told me that you are famous man in England and you are comed here to do very important works for Slavonicia.'

Although it was quite cool in the terminal, Pete suddenly realised that he was sweating again.

Irena took charge of Pete's case and guided him past the Customs and Immigration desk. An indignant official leapt out of his booth and started to remonstrate with them. Without breaking stride the young woman flashed a badge in a plastic holder in his face. The official immediately fell silent and retreated.

When Pete followed Irena through the terminal exit, he saw a large black limousine parked in front of a sign that read 'Nyet parksking'. A stocky, unsmiling chauffeur whose acne-scarred face resembled a long-distance shot of the moon's surface grabbed Pete's luggage. With surprising gentleness, the driver placed the case in the vehicle's cavernous boot.

'Me driver,' came a deep growl. 'Door not lock-ed. You getting in. Now!'

Pete thought it best not to argue. He climbed into the back of the ancient but roomy Russian Zil, a legacy of the previous régime, and settled back into the plush leather upholstery.

'We go now to hotel,' Irena informed him as she eased herself onto the bench seat next to him, displaying an expanse of shapely middle and, all too briefly as far as Pete was concerned, upper leg. Irena smoothed her skirt and turned to Pete.

'It is very modern hotel, best hotel in Bograd. In whole of Slavonicia, I think. I am sure that you will be pleasured there.'

She snapped out an instruction to the chauffeur. A moment later the Zil was speeding along the two-lane highway towards the capital. The driver was impressive; she managed, en route, to avoid almost every one of the potholes in the road.

Twenty-two

Bograd possesses neither the quaint, picture postcard charm of Prague, with its cobbled streets and gaily decorated façades, nor the unfeasibly broad boulevards and massive, brooding buildings of Budapest. As the limousine approached the city centre, Pete could see through its darkened windows people walking along slowly, heads downcast. They reminded him of the matchstick-like figures in an old framed print that his parents had had on their living-room wall.

The electric trams, even older than the ones he had seen on the occasional day-trip to Blackpool with his Auntie Jeannie, were full of glum-looking women wearing headscarves. As the trams clattered along, sparks shot forth from the overhead cables. As far as Pete could see, Bograd was a dump.

Half an hour after leaving the airport the Zil drew to a halt in front of the Grand Metropolitan Hotel in Demokratsmi Plazza, in the centre of Bograd. The hotel had been designed many decades earlier by the architect who had also been responsible for the Lubyanka prison in Moscow. Under the previous régime in Slavonicia, the Grand Metropolitan had fulfilled a similar function.

But all that belonged to the past. Shortly after declaring independence, the new Slavonician government, keen to make a statement showing its rejection of the bad old days, had ordered a major refurbishment of the granite monolith. The newly-created hotel now boasted, in addition to one hundred bedrooms, a restaurant and a swimming pool. In the hotel's basement was a gymnasium where, before the political upheaval, considerable numbers of Slavonicians had had their physical fitness tested rigorously and, in some cases, terminally.

Irena and Pete stepped inside the foyer and went towards the lift.

'Don't I need to, you know, check in or something?' asked Pete.

'Everything is already taken care of, Mr. Wasserman,' smiled Irena. 'Come with me; I take you to Presidential suite.'

They got out of the lift on the top floor. The young woman stopped outside the door of the suite and turned to Pete.

'I am sure you will finding everything you needing for your complete satisfaction. Servicing you in room is, naturally, available at any hour of the day' - she flashed him another smile - 'or night. I have gived instructions to manager that whatever you desire is to be provided immediately. But I am forgetful! Please be forgiving me. You are surely very fatigated after your lengthy travelling.'

The young woman unlocked the door and, ushering Pete into the suite, clapped her hands twice. Immediately the squat and extremely ugly female porter who had accompanied them in the elevator, and who looked as if in her younger days she might have been a useful middleweight wrestler, effortlessly lifted his heavy bag and deposited it on the king-sized bed. She hesitated for a moment, perhaps expecting a tip. A sharp word from the younger woman caused her to turn pale. Silently, she scurried away.

'I go now. You sleep,' said Irena. 'I come for you in hotel, tomorrow morning. We start, how you saying, early doorways, yes? Make sure you rest plenty much. You will needing all your energy.'

Pete was impressed by the splendour of the Presidential suite. He realised, with a mixture of amazement, pleasure and guilt that he was also quite taken with Irena.

'Listen, Irena. Seein' as we're gonna be workin' together, why don't you call me Pete?'

'OK,' she smiled. 'I am understanding. Thank you … Pete.'

She slipped the key to the Presidential suite into Pete's clammy hand, treated him to another radiant smile and closed the door softly behind her as she departed.

The following morning, Pete was sitting up in bed finishing the breakfast brought by room service. He supposed that Irena must have ordered it for him. He had never had beetroot jam on his toast before. Suddenly the bedside telephone rang shrilly.

'Yeh? Who is it?'

'Good morning, Mr. Wass … Pete.' Irena sounded a little breathless. The words came tumbling out.

'Did you slept well? I am so exciting! I come over now to show you what I got!'

*

Irena's sister Tatiana, Senior Secretary at the Ministry for Arts and Popular Culture was also excited by the file that she had put together on Pete Wasserman. Convinced that she was involved at the highest levels of government in a top-secret operation, the telephone conversations with her boyfriend had ceased abruptly. Now, whenever he tried to contact her, he was disappointed to find that she was unavailable.

Although Tatiana had always got on extremely well with Irena, her big sister told her very little about her work. Very well, then, thought Tatiana; she would just have to use her imagination and fill in the blanks. Pete Wasserman represented mystery, romance, perhaps even danger! The eighteen-year-old's imagination conjured up a world of international intrigue, midnight assignations, high-speed car chases in limousines with

121

bullet-proof windows – a heady mix of *Casablanca* and James Bond.

Showing a hitherto unseen degree of energy and initiative which astounded the Minister, Tatiana had taken to arriving early for work and leaving her desk just in time to catch the last tram home.

A week after beginning her research she proudly presented Irena with the fruits of her labour, a colour-coded, hand-drawn street map of Bograd. Tatiana had divided the capital into fifty-metre-square zones, each represented on a piece of A4 sized cardboard. The map, said Tatiana, would help Pete in his quest for the home-grown talent that, with the input of his own musical genius, would win the Eurovision Song Contest for Slavonicia.

Twenty-three

'Okay, Pete,' said Irena as she closed the door of the Presidential suite behind her. 'Where you want it? You like for me to spread on table?'

Before Pete could think of a reply the young woman unfastened her briefcase and took out the sections of the map.

'My little sister, Tatiana, she do this. She is clever girl, yes? no? We go into centre of Bograd. There is many cafés and bars where people sing in evening. It is like this in your country, yes, no? The beer in Slavonicia is very good, much gooder even than in Czech Republic. In my country people drink, they happy, they sing. We start tonight, yes, no?'

Pete found it difficult to cope with the barrage of double-barrelled questions. He wasn't sure whether to nod or shake his head but, when Irena spoke of people singing after sinking a few beers, he nodded enthusiastically; maybe this place wouldn't be too bad, after all.

'That's a great idea, Irena,' he replied. Pete looked at the watch he had bought at Argos the day after the visit from Slivovic. 'But it's only just gone eleven now. What are we gonna do for the rest of the day?'

'No worrying. I show you good time, Pete. I take you to places you never been. You will be amazing.'

Pete's heart was starting to pound again. The beautiful young woman looked directly into his eyes:

'I show you all famous sights of Bograd: Municipal Zoo, National Library, People's Theatre. I know you are man of great *cool-toor*. It will be be...' Irena frowned in concentration as she tried to recall the rather strange English expression that she had come across in one of the books she had read on her training course.

'It will be,' she beamed, suddenly remembering the phrase, 'right up your passage.'

*

At six o'clock the following morning, Pete's alcohol-enhanced slumber was interrupted by the strident ringing of the bedside phone. Eventually, his hand emerged from under the bedclothes and thrashed about in search of the offending instrument.

After the phone had rung a dozen times, Pete finally located the handset. Whoever was trying to get in touch with him at this hour of the morning was certainly persistent. They had better have a bloody good reason, he grumbled.

'Yeh?' he mumbled into the mouthpiece, 'Worrizit?'

'Good morning, Pete,' said Irena.

Pete wondered how she could manage to sound so bright that early in the day.

Clutching the phone and trying to stifle a yawn, he dragged himself out of bed, tripping over his clothes which were strewn all over the carpet. As Pete's head slowly cleared, memories of the previous evening trickled back into his brain. After visiting the sights of Bograd the previous day, he and Irena had spent the evening at a number of the capital's numerous watering holes, in their search for musical talent.

Pete had sat late into the night drinking litre tankards of lager with vodka chasers, watching all sorts of singers perform, in varying states of inebriation, the songs that had emptied thousands of karaoke bars all over the world. Hearing a Slavonician version of 'My Way' performed by a tattooed transvestite had certainly been a novel experience, especially when she/he had leered suggestively at Pete with the invitation to do it 'her/his way'. Despite the language barrier, the performer's body language had allowed no possible misunderstanding about what was on offer. Shuddering at the appalling memory, Pete dragged his thoughts back to the present.

'Where are you, Irena? Still at your flat?' he asked, hopefully. He yawned again. Christ, he thought, he was utterly wrecked. He needed more time to get his head together.

'No, Pete. I am already here, downstairs in lobby. You are coming down and joining me, yes?'

'OK, Irena. Just gimme a few minutes. Tell you what, why don't you have a coffee in the bar? I'll be there in two shakes.'

Pete hung up before she had a chance to ask him to explain the expression; there was only so much a man could cope with. Especially before he had had his breakfast.

*

Tatiana's map of Bograd had proved extremely useful; armed with comprehensive details of every café and bar in Bograd, Irena spent the next couple of weeks shepherding Pete around the capital.

Late one night, after several hours of having his ears assaulted by off-key crooners and tone-deaf warblers, Pete was sitting in his suite with Irena, who was gloomily sipping a coffee. Less than two months remained until the contest. His prospects of getting his hands on the half million quid that Slivovic had promised were receding by the day. Irena had been uncharacteristically quiet since they had got back to the hotel. Suddenly she leapt to her feet.

'Pete!' she exclaimed, clapping her hands with childlike glee, 'I have solv-ed problem!'

*

The double-page advertisement in the *Bograd People's Daily,* announcing a contest to discover a Slavonician singing superstar, attracted considerable interest. On the appointed day, dozens of people of all ages, sizes, shapes and genders, queued patiently outside the capital's Musikpalazz, tempted by the prospect of fame, fortune and a beetroot-free diet.

The first of the wannabees was a bouffanted blonde in her early thirties who was wearing too much make up. Pete reckoned that if you disregarded the slight paunch, the cylindrical legs and the hint of a moustache, she bore a passing resemblance to Dusty Springfield. The woman moved to the front of the stage and seized the microphone.

'Moo' - bellowed the bovine balladeer – 'na, reev air, why   darezan – amayal, eye – makross – eenyou eena – styal, samma - die.'

The beehived bombshell sang with great passion. There were even brief moments during her performance when she was in tune. After less than ten seconds Pete had heard enough.

'Thank you! Next!' he shouted. Irena interpreted. The blonde departed; tear-stained mascara traced a thin line down her cheeks.

Next on stage was an amateur opera singer, with powerful lungs and a chest of commensurate dimensions. The microphone was redundant. What a voice, thought Pete - but what an enormous arse!

'Thank you! Next!' Pete shouted again. The would-be diva glared at him as she flounced off the stage, mouthing imprecations which did not require Irena's interpreting skills.

Pete was revelling in his new role of pop impresario. He felt just like that guy who had had that programme on TV a few years back. What the hell was his name? It was on the tip of his tongue; Pete someone or other. He had been on the programme with that dolly bird, Michaela thingy. Pete recalled that he had quite fancied her at the time. But she hadn't been a patch on Tina. He suddenly realised just how much he was missing his wife.

Dozens more hopefuls followed; nearly all of them were hopeless. Only one, a pretty young girl of about sixteen with the body of an anorexic whippet and who was wearing a long-sleeved dress which fitted where it touched, displayed any real promise. The way she performed *Wind beneath my wings* showed an instinctive sense of the dramatic. Pete was excited: the girl was a natural!

Irena conveyed Pete's request for her to stay until the end of the session. When everyone else had left, Pete asked the girl to perform the song again.

'This time,' he suggested to the teenager, suiting his actions to his words, 'wave yer arms around a bit more, like! Toss yer 'ead back. And when yer hit the final note, lift yer arms right up and hold 'em out to the sides. Like you was flyin'. Gerrit?' Irena managed to convey the essence of Pete's advice.

With her long blond hair, pale complexion and eyes of china blue, the girl reminded Pete of the sixteen-year-old Marianne Faithfull by whom he had been captivated when she had appeared on *Top of the Pops* back in the early sixties. The girl's voice, powerful but with a catch in it that suggested an appealing vulnerability, had a touch of Edith Piaf.

Unfortunately, her resemblance to those two famous singers did not end there; it was only when the girl, following Pete's instructions, raised her hands aloft on the final, lingering note of the song that the sleeves of her shroud-like dress fell back to reveal the marks on her inner arms.

'Jesus Christ!' he exclaimed, turning to Irena. 'The kid's a fuckin' junkie!'

The Eurovision Song Contest was just four weeks away.

*

Back at the hotel Pete was unable to sleep. He brooded long into the night over the dilemma in which he now found himself. There was not enough time to go through the whole rigmarole of placing another advert and holding further auditions to find a suitable singer. That kid would have been perfect, he had told Irena. He had not come across a voice like that in ages.

Then he suddenly realised: Jesus! Not only had he not yet found a singer, he hadn't even written a song! The prospect of the half million quid receded even further. Pete's gloom deepened.

*

It was just after half-past three the following morning when the phone rang again.

'Pete! Pete! Wake up!' said the voice on the other end of the line. 'I got something I needing to tell you! Right now!'

'Izzat you, Irena? Do you know what time it is? Don't you ever sleep? Worrizit, anyway?'

'I have way we find new singer for contest.'

'It's impossible, Irena, love. There's not enough time. Even if ...'

Irena interrupted him; her tone was gentle but firm.

'Listen to what I got to say. I am just remembering about some of my friends from when I was at University here in Bograd. They were having no money to pay for vodka or books, so they were playing music at bars in evenings. My brother, Ivan, is friend of girl singer in group. Her name is Katerina. Ivan and Katerina are being very, how you say, lovey-dovey! The name they gived to their group it was Ivisniki. It is very old Slavonician word. It is meaning "songs in my chest". Ivan is saying to me one time that he think Katerina have many songs because she have so big chest. I smack him in mouth! He not saying that no more.'

Pete, now more or less awake, was just about managing to follow what Irena was saying. He knew better than to interrupt her; sooner or later she would get to the point.

'Anyways, Ivisniki music very popular in Bograd but they not making much money, so they ask friend to help them leave country. Now they living in London, in place called Breeks-ton. They doing cleaning jobs in day-time and singing in clubs in evening-time. Ivan tell me they making lots money because men always putting banknotes in Katerina's dress top. Is silly place for keeping money, yes, no? Anyways, I go phoning Ivan now.' The line went dead. Pete sighed deeply and pulled the quilt over his head.

He had just managed to get off to sleep when the phone rang again.

'I phone my sister Tatiana, too,' said Irena without further preamble. 'She fixing ticketings for you and me to go to Breeks-ton and see Ivisniki. We go today at cracking of dawn!'

Twenty-four

The streetlights had already been on for a couple of hours when the cab which had brought Pete and Irena from Heathrow deposited them outside a seedy-looking unit in a parade of shops in Brixton. By day, the ground floor of the premises was a greasy spoon café, patronised by poor, mainly immigrant customers.

After dark, however, it was the private club in the basement of the café that attracted a more affluent clientele. The establishment's patrons, having phoned their wives to say they had to work late at the office, trickled in from Westminster and the City. Its members, confident that there was virtually no possibility of their identity being revealed, enjoyed their respite from the tedious chores of making huge profits for multinational conglomerates or from pretending to govern the country.

The proprietor, the son of an émigré couple from Warsaw, had displayed impressive commercial acumen by diversifying into the entertainment industry; with no apparent sense of irony, he had named his lap-dancing club the Greasy Pole.

Irena looked around the area and wrinkled her nose in disapproval at the pavement strewn with empty cans and fast-food cartons.

'Is like… is like that word you use about my city when you comed to Bograd. Yes! I am remembering now! Sheet-house!'

As Pete and Irena stood in front of the entrance to the café, several men, their collars turned up and eyes cast down, hurried past them and went inside. One of them was wearing a woollen hat and black-framed glasses.

Pete overheard another well-dressed, middle-aged man speaking loudly into his mobile, promising the anxious-sounding voice on the other end that he would be back at the house in time for the division.

Pete didn't understand; he'd always thought division was something to do with sums. His puzzlement was interrupted by Irena.

'Pete,' she whispered urgently, 'we must go in now. People start looking at us!'

Outside the club, a large, shaven-headed doorman barred their way.

'Sorry, love. Members only.'

Irena took two fifty-pound notes from her purse and fluttered them in the bouncer's face.

'We new members, is OK?'

The doorman grabbed the banknotes and stood aside to let them pass before following them inside. In their haste to get into the club, neither Pete nor Irena noticed a man in a black leather jacket who was speaking animatedly into his mobile.

The subterranean room was small, cold and damp. There were several round tables arranged in a circle. In the centre, to the tinny accompaniment of pre-recorded music, a bored-looking girl was gyrating around a pole. From time to time a ten pound note found its way from the hand of one of the anonymous customers into her scanty clothing. A few minutes later the music suddenly stopped and the girl wandered off to the sanctuary of her dressing-room.

The bouncer, who had undergone a rapid transformation into the club's compère, grabbed a microphone.

'And now,' he began.

A voice in the darkness called out: 'the end is near!'

'Shat yer fice, smartarse!' said the bouncer, glaring into the darkness as he tried in vain to locate the wag. Having recovered his composure, he continued:

'On stige now, gennulmen, we praardly present the light-est moosical sens-eye-shun, all the wye from Slav .. Slavi.. Anywye, put yer 'ands an' feet togevver for: Ivisniki!'

From behind a curtain two young women and a man shuffled out onto the small stage on which stood a drum kit and an electric keyboard. Irena noticed that the keyboard player's blond hair had grey roots and that she was wearing too much make-up. The drummer was much younger and prettier. It wasn't hard to work out which one was Katerina. The third member of the group was Irena's brother, Ivan.

Irena's command of English was not shared by her sibling; without any preliminaries, Ivan turned to the drummer and mouthed: "Un-ya, du-ya, tru-ya, quat-ya!" before launching into a heavily accented version of a song that had topped the charts several months before.

For a couple of minutes Pete listened to the group but did not say a word. Irena looked at him with concern. Had they come all this way, she wondered, for nothing?

Pete, his foot tapping in time to the music, suddenly turned to Irena, smiling:

'I think we might be in luck, this time!'

*

As the members of Ivisniki emerged from the Greasy Pole, Irena rushed up to her brother and flung her arms around his neck. In rapid Slavonician she explained in detail why she and Pete had come to London.

'So,' she summarised for Pete, 'I explaining to Ivan and two girls that three days from today we all going back together to Bograd to learn new song you writing for contest, special for them. I tell them they will be rich and famous. They no need to be playing in places like this sheet-house. I tell them we must be meeting at Heathrow airport at eleven hours, sharply. They is all very exciting.'

Irena continued to talk excitedly with her brother. Pete could make out only one word, 'Oleg', as Ivan, smiling, gave his sister the thumbs up. She nodded enthusiastically.

After informing the proprietor of the club where he could stick his greasy pole, the three musicians disappeared into the Brixton night in search of a more salubrious place in which to celebrate their good fortune.

The owner was furious; business had boomed while Ivisniki had been performing at the club. Lap-dancers were ten a penny, but a good band was hard to find. Swearing vengeance, he cursed the three of them loudly in his mother tongue as they left his premises for the last time.

For the first time since he had embarked on his mission Pete was feeling confident; this group, he had seen and heard, was half-way decent. In the short time remaining before the contest he would be able to teach them a few tricks of the musical trade. There remained only the small matter of writing a song for Europe.

*

Three days later Pete and Irena, after checking in at the Air France desk at Heathrow, were waiting for the three band members to show up. Their flight for Paris, the first leg of the journey to Bograd, had just been called. There was still no sign of the members of Ivisniki.

Five minutes later another announcement came over the public address system: 'This is the last and final call for Air France flight AF 007 for Paris Charles de Gaulle. Will all remaining passengers for this flight please go immediately to Gate 26.'

Pete looked anxiously at his watch.

'Where the hell are they, Irena?' he muttered. 'They should have been here ages ago.'

Irena, for once, also seemed worried as she scanned the terminal, looking for her brother and his friends.

Suddenly she screamed and started to jump up and down like a teenage fan at a pop concert.

'Look, Pete! Ivan and girls, over there!'

'Ivan!' she shouted, waving her arms in the air, 'We are here! Hurry up, we are late for plane!'

Irena's brother and his two fellow musicians ambled over with no particular sense of urgency.

'Come on, Ivan!' she cried. 'You must be checking in, quick sticks!'

'Is OK, Irena,' he replied, unconcerned. 'We been collecting passports from Oleg. He fix everything, no problem.' He gave his sister a conspiratorial wink.

'When youse two have finished chatting,' interrupted Pete, 'we've gorra plane to catch.' Turning to Ivan, he said: 'You lot had better get yourselves checked in, right now.'

Ivan strolled up to the young woman at the check-in desk and favoured her with what he regarded as a winning smile.

'May I see your passport, sir?' asked the official. Still smiling, he handed her the shiny new document. The woman held it next to a machine. Her frown was almost imperceptible. After a few seconds she said, brightly:

'Would you mind waiting here, sir? I shan't keep you a moment.'

She left her desk and went into a back room where she picked up a phone and began to speak animatedly. Every few seconds she looked through the window to check that he was still there and smiled reassuringly. Ivan was beginning to fancy his chances with the check-in girl.

His optimism did not last long. Without warning four uniformed, armed policemen surrounded Ivan and his fellow-musicians. The man who was obviously the senior member of the quartet addressed Irena's brother:

'I have reason to believe that you and your companions are in breach of United Kingdom immigration laws.' He reeled off with practised ease a list of the relevant sections and sub-sections. With exaggerated courtesy he invited them to accompany him to the police station. Each of his fellow officers endorsed this invitation by seizing one of the members of Ivisniki by an arm.

Pete was dumbfounded. 'What d'yer mean? What's goin' on?'

The senior officer explained: 'My department is acting on an anonymous tip-off. Our informant was extremely upset; he was most insistent on doing his civic duty and was very specific in his allegations. It would appear that these persons' - he pointed to Ivan and his two fellow-musicians - 'have been attempting to use forged travel documents. The young lady at the check-in reported that the passport presented by this gentleman' - he indicated Irena's brother – 'is indeed a fake. A very good one, it must be said, but a forgery nonetheless.'

He turned to one of his colleagues. 'Right, Cunningham,' he said briskly, 'let's get these characters out of here, and with as little fuss as possible.'

Pete could not believe what was happening. He turned to Irena.

'Did you know they was illegals? Why didn't you tell me before? Now we're fucked good and proper!'

'But Pete, *everybody* who is coming to London from my country is illegal! They pay money to Albanian gangster. He is bringing them in truck. He is saying no-one needing passport! Ivan and the others are here since one year, no problems.'

'Well there's a problem now, all right!'

Irena had never seen Pete like this. Blinking back her tears, she was determined to be positive:

'We are finding way, Pete. Anyway, you and me we are getting on plane now. Ivan and the girls will be OK. I talk to my sister, Tatiana. She talk to her boss - he fix everything. But now we get on plane; when we are arriving in Bograd, we are thinking of new plan.'

*

135

During the several stages of the long journey back to Bograd, Pete dozed fitfully. Every few minutes he woke up in a sweat, wondering just how the hell he was going to find a band to replace Ivisniki. And even if he did, how could he possibly write a song and rehearse it in time? Only one week remained until the finals of the Eurovision Song Contest.

Twenty-five

The meeting between Sir Douglas Anstruther and the President of Slavonicia had been a great success. The diplomat, comprehensively briefed by MI6, who knew all about his guest's appreciation of the finer things in life, had provided a sumptuous dinner at his private residence, just round the corner from Carlton Square Gardens.

Lady Magdalena had surpassed herself; her choice of Scottish smoked salmon, Scotch broth, followed by Aberdeen Angus fillet steak flambé topped with haggis had all been greatly appreciated by their epicurean visitor. The vintage wines selected to accompany each course had also received their distinguished guest's enthusiastic approval. Magdalena basked in the President's effusive compliments.

'That is so kind of you, President Sonofábic,' she purred. 'It has been such a delightful evening but I fear that one of my migraines is coming on,' she lied. 'If you will excuse me I shall go and lie down in my room.'

The President and her husband stood as she left the dining room, pausing only to pick up her newspaper and a large box of chocolates from the sofa in the lounge before going into her bedroom. The door closed softly behind her.

As the President sat back contentedly in one of the Hepplewhite chairs, Sir Douglas leaned forward and poured into his guest's glass a second generous measure of his private stock of fifty-year-old Courvoisier. He judged that the moment had come to broach the subject that he had raised at the conference earlier that day.

'Mr. President,' he began, tentatively.

'I think that in view of the splendid hospitality that you and your charming wife have shown me we could perhaps dispense with formalities, don't you agree? Please call me Fyodor.'

'Ah, yes, er, quite. Certainly … er… Fyodor. Oh, and, er, please do call me Douglas.'

The cognac was having a beneficial effect. This was such a more civilised way to do business, reflected Sir Douglas as he, too, savoured the vintage brandy. He recalled with distaste the frequent occasions long ago in the 1960s when, as a very junior government official, he had been despatched by that appalling little man Wilson to obtain bottles of brown ale and ham sandwiches, when the Prime Minister had been trying to placate trade union leaders at Number Ten.

The President was no fool; there was no such thing, he knew perfectly well, as a free lunch – or a free dinner, for that matter. Fyodor Sonovábic owed his success – indeed, his survival – to his ultra-sensitive political antennae. It was clear that Anstruther was a master of his craft. The man had some ulterior motive, but what? The President decided to probe.

'That was truly a memorable dinner, Douglas. You must ask your wife to let me have the recipe for the soup. It was delicious.'

Sir Douglas inclined his head slightly, acknowledging the compliment. He neglected to inform his Excellency, the President of the People's Independent State of Slavonicia, that his wife had bought it, as well as all the other items they had enjoyed that evening, at the local Tesbury's a few days previously. Although she and Sir Douglas were now very comfortably off, Magdalena had retained the thriftiness instilled in her by her mother during her upbringing in Penuria. Magdalena timed her trips to the supermarket to coincide with the appearance on the reduced counter of those items of food that had reached their sell-by date.

'You are too generous, Fyodor,' responded Sir Douglas. 'I shall certainly tell my wife. I know that your kind words will give her considerable pleasure.'

There was a pause. The President looked at him keenly. 'I sense that perhaps there is something that is troubling you, Douglas. You appear to be a little, er, what is the word, pre-occupied. Perhaps I may be of assistance?'

'Well, since you mention it, Fyodor, there *is* something that has occurred to me. It's just a minor matter - hardly worth talking about, really.'

The diplomat smiled at his guest. It would be better not to rush into this. The oblique approach would be best, starting with a change of subject.

'I must say, Fyodor, strictly off the record, of course, that I really do sympathise with you over that foreign aid business with the Americans. It was damnably mean of them to turn down your entirely reasonable request for that thousand-year interest-free loan. Naturally, we tried our very best during the break in the Security Council meeting in New York last week to make them see the situation from your point of view. But you know what the Yanks are like – only interested in what's in it for them; they never spare a thought for the other chap. Just between the two of us, I think they're cutting back on foreign aid because they're looking for an excuse to get more involved in the Middle East and they need to channel more money into their armed forces. They're worried about just one thing – oil. I wouldn't put it past them to invade some country in that part of the world, one of these days, on some pretext or other.'

Sir Douglas judged that the moment had now come to broach the subject about which he had been speaking earlier that day to the European Heads of State.

'Yes, Fyodor, since you mention it, there *is* something which I should very much like to discuss with you. Something which, when you've heard it, I am sure you will agree will be of great benefit to Slavonicia, as well as to the European Community.'

'As I am sure you are well aware, Douglas,' interjected the President dryly, 'Slavonicia does not belong to that esteemed fraternity.'

'Ah, yes, Fyodor. I shall come back to that, er, issue in a moment. But first let me share with you what I have in mind. I think that you will find it interesting. Very interesting indeed.'

*

'So Fyodor,' summarised Sir Douglas. 'your government would give us, I mean of course NATO, the go-ahead to establish a military base in Slavonicia – and I hardly need to tell you, my friend, just how many thousands of jobs that would create for your economy - and we, for our part, should lend you our most emphatic support in your application for membership of the European Community.'

Sir Douglas smiled as he continued. 'You know, Fyodor, we British may have lost an Empire but we believe that we still have a certain part to play in international affairs. With such a proposal as I have outlined, everyone would benefit. There would be no losers – except, of course,' Sir Douglas permitted himself the briefest chuckle, 'for the Barakistanis! Slavonicia will prosper' – Sir Douglas felt sufficiently emboldened to switch from the conditional tense to the future - 'and you, my dear Fyodor, will be hailed as the guarantor of world peace. Your place in history will be assured. I am certain that when you hold your next election in, if I remember correctly, six months from now, the Slavonician people will not have forgotten your outstanding achievements on their behalf. But enough of that! Let me tempt you to another glass of this really rather splendid brandy. And perhaps, afterwards, you would also care to let me have your opinion of this.'

Sir Douglas unlocked a drawer in his bureau and took out a small brown paper packet.

'It arrived this morning in the Diplomatic bag. Direct from Colombia.'

*

The President smiled at his host.

'As I am sure you are already well aware, Douglas,' he said, 'I am a great Anglophile.'

The President's speech, although slightly slurred, had lost none of its fluency. Sir Douglas recalled one Eastern European Head of State whose notorious inability to hold his drink had saved the British secret services a considerable amount of costly and quite probably dangerous work.

Sir Douglas made encouraging noises. The President continued:

'When I was much younger, I spent several months here at one of your, how do you call them, redbrick universities. It was a most interesting period of my life but, sadly, I had to cut short my studies in order to return home.'

Sir Douglas was well aware of the reason for the premature departure from the United Kingdom of the future President of Slavonicia. The briefing from MI6 had referred to the young Sonofábic having engaged in 'activities incompatible with his student status.' Douglas nodded sympathetically. All that had been in the past, a long, long time ago. Yesterday's deadly enemies were today's most intimate friends. Such was the world of international politics.

The President inhaled appreciatively. Now fully relaxed, he was ready to impart more personal confidences to his host.

'I am having one or two little problems with my daughter, Petrushka. She is nineteen, a very clever girl. And what is more she is beautiful. Just like her dear mother, may she rest in peace.'

The President's eyes were filling with emotion. He took an Irish linen handkerchief from his pocket and blew noisily into it before continuing. 'But I am afraid that my daughter is also somewhat, what shall I say, spirited. Since my wife died five years ago she has become increasingly difficult to control. Even the most awkward members of my government are as small children compared to my darling Petrushka.'

He sighed deeply before continuing.

'A few months ago I decided to send her to study for a year in England. I thought that spending some time in a sober, academic environment would help her to settle down. When she last spoke to me on the telephone, several weeks ago, she said how much she was enjoying student life. She was even managing, she said, to do some studying. But, sadly, all has not gone according to plan. I have recently been informed that Petrushka has got into some difficulties in which certain, er, substances were involved. It seems that she has fallen in with a bad crowd of young men who attended one of your most famous public schools.' He named it. 'Naturally, I am sure that she is entirely innocent of any wrong-doing. However, the Master of her college has indicated that he is going to be obliged to - what is the word he used? - rusticate her. That is the reason for my visit to your country, as a private citizen. The college disciplinary hearing is to take place tomorrow morning.' His voice faltered. 'I must do everything I can for my little girl. You have children, Douglas?' The President did not wait for a response. 'Then you will understand, I am sure, a father's feelings.'

The Scot nodded in sympathy with his guest. He enquired gently:

'Where is your daughter studying? Perhaps I might be able to help. I still have one or two contacts in academic circles.'

'She is at Oxford University, St. Judas's College. Do you know it?'

The expression on Douglas's face did not alter.

'Yes, indeed I do, Fyodor. It so happens that the current Master of St. Judas's and I were up together.'

The President looked at him questioningly.

'Oh, I'm so sorry, Fyodor. Forgive me. I meant that the Head of St. Judas's, Octavian Blenkinsop, and I were fellow-students at the college many years ago.'

Douglas paused to refresh his memory. He remembered Blenkinsop as being an averagely bright lad from some small mill town or other in the North West of England; Accrington, was it, or perhaps Blackburn? Anyway, it was of no consequence. He looked directly into the President's eyes.

'Perhaps I might be able to prevail upon my old friend Octavian to see your daughter's situation in a different light.'

Sir Douglas looked at his watch and smiled.

'Good. I rather suspect that he'll be back in his lodgings by now. Octavian Blenkinsop is a creature of habit. He always works late after High Table – sorry, Fyodor, that is to say after dinner. Now might be a propitious moment to contact him. Perhaps you would excuse me for a brief moment?'

Sir Douglas went into his study, closing the door behind him. He opened a locked drawer in his bureau, took out a black leather-bound book and consulted it briefly before dialling an ex-directory Oxford number.

'Octavian? It's Douglas here. Yes, my friend, Douglas Anstruther. Yes, fine thank you. Yes, a long time, indeed. But I'm sure that you, of all people, appreciate the heavy burdens of office. I'm so sorry to disturb you at such a late hour, but I knew that you would be occupied with College affairs after High Table. Dedicated people such as you never rest. I remember that Margaret was just the same when she was at Number Ten.'

In the background, Douglas could hear the familiar theme tune of a television soap opera. Blenkinsop, he knew, was a devotee of Coronation Street; he was no doubt watching the recording of the current episode whose screening earlier that evening would have coincided with High Table. The Scot smiled to himself before continuing.

'But let me to come straight to the point, Octavian. It's really a rather trifling matter. I do so hate to trouble you with it. There seems to have been a misunderstanding involving one of your undergraduates, a lassie from one of these faraway foreign places. Slavonicia, I think it's called. The girl's name is Petrushka Sonovábic. I understand that she's got herself into a spot of bother and I was wondering ...'

...

'Well, Octavian, you are of course perfectly correct. Naturally, there cannot be any exceptions. Rules, as you so profoundly say, are rules. However, I know something of the girl's family. It's really a rather sad case. Her mother died tragically young. The daughter was deeply affected by her death. In fact, she has never really recovered. I have it on excellent authority that, despite the present, er, unfortunate circumstances, she is in fact a sweet, gentle girl, as well as being – as I'm sure you are aware, Octavian - extremely able. I imagine she must be a real asset to the college, academically. There are so few real high fliers these days, aren't there? Not like in our day, eh, Octavian? In fact, and at the risk of seeming immodest, you and I were the only two men of real ability when we were undergraduates together at St. Judas's.'

...

'Yes, Octavian, I know that even the brightest must conform to the rules. But, as you yourself often used to say so wisely, circumstances alter cases. I was wondering, therefore, whether ...'

...

'Well, of course, I understand completely that your hands are tied. It's such a pity, however, what with the New Year's Honours list coming up. Your name has been mentioned more than once. If it were my decision, I should warmly support your elevation to the Lords. It would be a fitting reward for all your long years of devoted, selfless service.'

...

'Bribe you? Really! My dear Octavian! How could you think such a thing of me?! I am most offended! When I recall that recent deplorable business with the brown envelope in which you were implicated. Why, only last week I had a phone call from a reporter from one of the tabloids. I was able to put him off, not without some difficulty, I might add. But you know how persistent these fellows can be.'

Sir Douglas paused for a few seconds before adding: 'It might not be possible, next time.'

...

'Very well, I accept your apology. But perhaps you might be minded to reconsider your decision?'

...

'Yes, the list is due to be presented to the PM next week, before it is submitted to Her Majesty for her approval.'

...

'I can foresee no difficulty with that suggestion, Octavian. Yes, indeed; I do agree that Lord Blenkinsop of Oswaldtwistle has a rather splendid ring to it!'

...

'Well, Octavian, that's very good of you. I do appreciate this. And rest assured, your generosity of spirit will not go unnoticed in the appropriate quarters.'

...

'Don't mention it. No, Octavian.' Sir Douglas' voice had taken on a firmer tone. 'I really do mean that, quite literally. You must not breathe a word of this to a soul.'

Confident that he had achieved his objective, he reverted to his earlier conversational manner.

'No, not even to All Souls! Ha! Ha! Goodnight, Octavian. Or, at the risk of seeming premature, may I say ... *Lord* Blenkinsop? But I must not take up any more of your valuable time. Good night, Octavian.'

Sir Douglas replaced the handset in its cradle and returned to his guest. Smiling, he gently patted the shoulder of the anxious President.

'I think I can reassure you, Fyodor, that your daughter's situation will be resolved to your satisfaction.'

The President looked at Sir Douglas with renewed respect.

'Thank you so much, my dear friend. I shall not forget your kindness.' He consulted his Rolex Oyster. 'It is late. I must go, but...'

Sir Douglas noted the President's hesitancy.

'What is the matter, Fyodor?'

'I regret very much, but there is one further favour I must ask of you. It is not a personal matter, this time, but rather one that is of immense significance for the national pride of Slavonicia. However, I fear that my request may be beyond the scope of even your considerable talents.'

Sir Douglas' curiosity was aroused; he relished a challenge.

'What is it, my friend? Just tell me.'

The President told him.

*

As soon as the President had left, Sir Douglas went into the bedroom where his wife, propped up on several pillows, was watching television as she steadily worked her way through the large box of chocolates which had been on special offer at the petrol station.

'Thank you so much my dear,' he said, 'for giving Fyodor and myself the opportunity to discuss politics; I know how boring you find it. But to change the subject completely, I'd like to pick your brains about something.'

'Yes, dear?' enquired his wife distractedly, her attention focused on the latest episode of *Eastenders* which she had recorded earlier that evening.

'Could you explain something about the arrangements for the voting in the Eurovision Song Contest? Fyodor and I were chatting about various matters after dinner, and the subject came up. It seems that he is quite a fan and I must confess that I found myself at a disadvantage.'

'Arrangements?' queried Lady Magdalena. 'You make it sound as though it's all been fixed in advance!'

Her husband laughed. 'You *are* amusing, my dear; I've always loved your sense of humour.'

'It's really quite straightforward,' she continued, without taking her eyes from the television screen. Sir Douglas's wife pointed to an occasional table on which there was a colour supplement from the previous edition of *Excess on Saturday*. 'It's all explained in this article; why don't you read it?'

She took another chocolate from the box before turning her attention back to the life-and-death dramas that were the staple diet of the inhabitants of Albert Square. As Lady Magdalena bit into another crème caramel, she reflected that no matter how bad a day she had endured, she could take comfort in the fact that theirs was infinitely worse.

*

Sir Douglas went into his study, sat down at his desk and started to read the magazine article. It had been written by an Irish television presenter, Kerry Hogan, who provided a whimsical appraisal of each of the entries for the forthcoming contest. Sir Douglas was interested to see that across the double-page spread there appeared in neat columns the name of each competing country, a photograph of the performer who was going to represent it and the title of the song. There was also a brief explanation of the voting procedure and a profile of the chairperson of the jury for each participating country.

The details of the songs and the performers were not of the slightest interest to Sir Douglas. As he perused the article a plan rapidly took shape in his mind. He smiled as he recalled an essay he had written as an undergraduate on the subject of random numbers. His eyes narrowed as he made some rapid calculations. Yes! It *could* be done!

Sir Douglas took a sheet of writing paper from a drawer of his bureau. In one column, he copied down from the magazine an alphabetical list of the competing countries. Then he drew a series of thin pencil lines, connecting each country with several others. Next to the name of each country he jotted down a series of digits. After twenty minutes he put down his pencil: in principle his plan would work.

Sir Douglas was well aware that what he had just done was the easy part of the plan; the next step was critical and would require the most careful use of his diplomatic skills.

From another drawer of his bureau he extracted a thick, leather-bound ring-binder. Sir Douglas referred to it as his Book of Revelations. He had got the idea many years earlier from a former colleague who worked in the Government Whips' office.

With the occasional assistance of junior members of the security services, whose moonlighting activities he discreetly rewarded, Sir Douglas regularly updated his records of the guilty secrets of politicians and other public figures. Within the pages of the binder could be found details of adulterous liaisons involving libidinous Members of Parliament and their invariably young and attractive 'researchers', some of whom were female. Nor had the cocaine addiction of an eminent Law Lord, whose regular anti-drug tirades were frequently reported in the media, escaped his attention.

Sir Douglas's antennae extended far beyond the shores of the United Kingdom; he had noted the penchant of the senior Senator of one of the more conservative southern States of America for entertaining underage black girls. The 'casting couch' promotion system, energetically embraced by the Minister for Equal Opportunities of one of the United Kingdom's closest European allies, also had been scrupulously logged.

Everyone, in Sir Douglas' long experience, had a skeleton in their cupboard; consequently, everyone could be bought. The only variation lay in the nature of the currency to be used.

Sir Douglas opened the ring-binder, the leather cover creaking gently as he pressed the pages flat. He unscrewed the cap of his Parker 51 fountain pen, a gift from his father for having gained a scholarship to Edinburgh Academy, and took a fresh sheet of stiff, hole-punched cartridge paper from the reserve stock at the back of the binder. The only information he needed to enter was a coded reference to the person and to his or her country. He smiled as, at the top of the page, he wrote in firm, bold capitals the phrase he had devised for the entry that he was about to make. Sir Douglas wrote steadily for several minutes in his minute hand before closing the volume and returning it to the drawer of the bureau which he locked.

To the ordinary reader, the contents of the black binder would have been incomprehensible. They made sense only to their writer, who had retained his penchant for obscure, punning allusions. The language was that of the Times cryptic crossword compiler of yesteryear. Sir Douglas was confident that there was no possibility of anyone being able to work out the clue: 'male canine offspring - urine'. He smiled again at the ring-binder with its newly added reference to Sonovábic, the President of the People's Independent State of Slavonicia.

The diplomat looked at the sheet on which he had listed the countries that were due to be taking part in the contest. He then turned to another page in the ring binder. On it, some months previously, he had written some notes concerning the Head of State of one of those countries. Sir Douglas smiled as he refreshed his memory before picking up the handset of his scrambler phone and dialling a long number. It was going to be an even longer night.

Twenty-six

In the trees near Carlton House Terrace the birds were clearing their throats in preparation for the dawn chorus. With a sigh of contentment Sir Douglas replaced the handset after making his final call of the night.

Almost every one of the national leaders whom he had contacted during the preceding hours had been soundly asleep when their phones had rung. Any initial displeasure at having their slumber disturbed quickly evaporated when Sir Douglas explained the reason for his call. Should it prove necessary, he informed them, they might wish to make use of the highly confidential information with which he was about to entrust them. The people he was asking them to contact should be told, added the Scot, that what they were being requested to do would be in the long-term interests of their country.

During the following twenty-four hours, all but one of the persons whom Sir Douglas had asked the leaders to contact did not require the consequences of their unwillingness to co-operate to be spelt out.

The exception was a household name in the media whose son was, unknown to the general public of his country, a bisexual alcoholic with a gambling problem. Faced with an initial resistance to his request, the national leader, primed by Sir Douglas, expressed the sincere hope that the young man's issues, if they were leaked, would not prove to be an impediment to his budding political career. Compliance followed immediately

Sir Douglas, stifling a yawn, could not prevent himself from smiling as the words of the former American President, Lyndon Johnson, came to his mind: "When you've got them by the balls," the Texan Machiavelli had been in the habit of saying, "their hearts and minds will follow."

This testicular reference reminded Douglas of the time many years earlier when, as a student on holiday in Sicily, he had had his possessions stolen by two young bandits, only for them to be returned to him with interest thanks to the intervention of Giuseppe who, subsequently, he had discovered to be his future wife's brother. 'Of *course*!' he exclaimed, 'Why didn't I think of it before? Giuseppe!'

*

'I've been thinking, my dear,' said the diplomat. 'It's been quite some time since we've spoken with your brother. Perhaps it might be an idea to phone him and see how he and his family are keeping. Now might be a convenient time to reach him; he'll be having breakfast.'

'Dear Douglas,' smiled Magdalena, 'that is *so* thoughtful of you! You are always thinking of other people, never about yourself.' She kissed him on the cheek. 'That is why I love you so much.'

Douglas dialled the number of his brother-in-law at his family estate in the countryside not far from Palermo. Giuseppe had realised his ambition of reclaiming his parents' property by marrying the daughter of the man who had bought it from them at a price far below its market value.

Giuseppe and his wife, happily married for many years, had been as fertile as their land; they had produced seven children, all of whom were involved in the family-owned olive oil business.

Douglas and Giuseppe had kept in regular touch over the years, sometimes speaking in the Sicilian's dialect, a feat which had continued to impress Magdalena.

The Scot concealed his impatience while his wife and her brother chatted about family matters. When she had finally run out of news, Magdalena held out the phone to her husband. Managing to contain a sigh of relief he started to talk with Giuseppe.

After exchanging the usual greetings, Douglas broached the subject which was the real reason for his call.

'I wonder, Giuseppe, if perhaps you could help me with a small problem which is proving to be a little tricky?' The diplomat elaborated. 'There is a person here in England who needs to be persuaded to perform a task which he might find impossible to agree to in normal circumstances. He could be contacted by phone, but it is essential that the call should not be made from my own country. I can provide you with some helpful information which you might need to use to, er, encourage him to do as he is asked.'

Giuseppe listened in silence while his brother-in-law outlined his scheme. He did not ask for any explanation from the man who had saved his life some forty years before. The Sicilian remembered the promise he had made at the time, that he would do anything that Douglas might ask of him. He was a man of his word.

*

Sir Douglas had almost forgotten; there remained just one further call that he needed to make. He looked at his watch. The previous evening – it seemed such a long time ago – Sir Douglas had apologised to the president of Slavonicia for his Prime Minister's absence. The PM, Sir Douglas had informed his guest, had been called away at the last minute to a secret congress that would require his input. The Premier had asked Sir Douglas to convey his sincere regrets but hoped that ... blah, blah, blah.

The Prime Minister, as Sir Douglas was well aware, was in fact ensconced in a love nest in the Swiss Alps;

the congress in question was with a young, beautiful and extremely discreet secretary from his Private Office at Number Ten. The thought that he might, with any luck, be interrupting his leader's input at a particularly critical moment brought a flicker of a smile to the diplomat's features as he punched into the scrambler phone the digits of the PM's top-secret mobile number.

Twenty-seven

According to tradition the Finals of the Eurovision Song Contest were staged in the country which had produced the previous year's winner. The Italian seaside town of Positaro, which had been chosen to stage the event, was preparing with great excitement.

The song which had brought fame and the hope of prosperity to this small Adriatic resort had been performed by a harmony duo from Venice. Their offering had been a novelty song, sung in heavily accented English accompanied by Presleyesque pelvic thrusts. Not wishing to be thought of by their fellow-Europeans as lacking a sense of humour, most of the judges had entered into the spirit of the proceedings and awarded the outstandingly appalling composition the maximum 'douze points'. Having been dismissed as a no-hoper before the contest by the assembled musical *cognoscenti*, the song had duly won by a landslide.

*

In Bograd, Pete shut himself away in his hotel suite and concentrated on the task of composing a song that would take Europe by storm. After a twelve-hour stint all he had to show for his efforts was a bedroom floor littered with crumpled sheets of paper and a splitting headache. He looked at his watch. It was just after midnight. He badly needed a drink.

He found the lounge bar deserted, apart from a couple of young waiters who were chatting as they cleared away the empty glasses from the tables. Earlier in the evening, a three piece band had been playing; the piano, drum kit and double-bass were still on the small raised platform.

One of the waiters, taking a break from clearing up the mess, went over and picked up the drumsticks. He started to tap out a catchy beat. He wasn't bad at all, thought Pete.

The other waiter, older than his colleague, started to pluck the strings of the double-bass. He, too, seemed to know what he was doing; together, the two of them were producing a half-decent rhythm. It was a pity, thought Pete, that it was so late and that he was feeling so knackered, otherwise he would have sat in with them on the piano and they could have had a bit of a jam session.

It was getting on for one o'clock. Pete, yawning, decided to go back up to his suite and try to get a few hours' sleep. He got undressed and emptied his trouser pockets onto the bed. Out of his wallet fell a jumble of banknotes and an old black and white photograph of Tina. He picked up the faded snapshot and looked at it; he had taken it with his Brownie box camera almost forty years earlier, shortly after they had started going out together. He had always carried it with him. The teenage girl was smiling, without a care in the world. Pete stared at the photograph for a long time. Suddenly, he realised what he had to do.

*

Each year, on a Saturday evening in May, millions of British television viewers settled themselves in front of their set with a cup of tea and looked forward to watching the Eurovision Song Contest. Many of them were far less interested in the musical offerings of Europe's finest than in what Kerry Hogan would have to say during the course of the evening.

The genial Dubliner had been presenting the Eurovision for British television viewers for as long as anyone, including himself, could remember. Discordant harmonies, uncoordinated choreography and sartorial disasters – nothing escaped the Irishman's barbed comments, delivered in a deceptively gentle brogue.

A similar fate awaited under-rehearsed singers, tongue-tied fellow-presenters or arithmetically-challenged juries who cast their votes incorrectly. It was highly likely on the evidence of previous contests that at some point in the proceedings there would be a cock-up.

All of this was meat and drink to Kerry. As he took a sip from a glass of mineral water, he looked forward to another routine but enjoyable evening of extracting the Michael from hapless performers and, if the opportunity arose, from colleagues, too.

*

'And now, fellow sufferers, we come to the entry from Slavonicia, performed by...' – through the bifocals perched on the end of his nose, Kerry Hogan looked at his notes - 'ah, now let me see; there appears to have been a last-minute change to the schedule. Ivisniki, a trio which was to have represented Slavonicia, has had to withdraw at the last minute due to unforeseen circumstances. The last time I came across that excuse, it was a sign on a fortune-teller's booth! Anyway, it seems that the group's travel arrangements have been disrupted and, unfortunately, they are unable to be present to perform tonight. In their place, the People's Independent State of Slavonicia, to give the country its full title, will be represented by one Pete Wasserman who, I am given to understand, hails from Liverpool, of all places.'

Hogan consulted his notes again.

'It's been a few years now since Slavonicia last took part in the Eurovision. On their last – indeed, their only - previous appearance, the Slavonician entry achieved the distinction of being awarded the dreaded 'nul points'. So, in the words of the auld song, the only way is up! Well, now, let's see if this expatriate Scouser is going to produce a brand new Mersey sound.'

Kerry Hogan put a finger to his ear.

'Ah! I can hear me producer whisperin' in me shell-like. I think we're all ready now to hear what Slavonicia has to offer this time round. So, let's settle back and listen to Pete Wasserman as he performs his very own composition: Tina.'

There was a polite smattering of applause as Pete emerged from the wings onto the darkened stage of the Positaro Lido. Behind him were his backing musicians - the two waiters from the hotel.

The morning after he had seen them in the hotel bar, Pete learned from Irena that they had formerly been students at the St Petersburg Conservatoire. Due to lack of funds they had had to abandon their studies and return to Slavonicia. Irena had explained Pete's predicament and had persuaded them that if they would accompany Pete they could assure not only their own future but that of their nation. The two musicians had agreed at once.

Suddenly, a single spotlight focused on Pete. The audience in the auditorium fell silent at the sight of the tubby, middle-aged man who stood before them, holding a battered-looking ukulele.

Pete moved his head closer to the microphone, counted in his backing musicians and started to strum his instrument. In the audience, feet began to tap in time with the simple, plonking rhythm which was totally different from any of the other over-produced rubbish that had been heard that evening. The lyrics, too, had an air of innocence, as if they were being sung by a love-struck teenager rather than by a man in his fifties.

The lyrics were different from those that Pete had originally written more than thirty years earlier; the song was now about his lost love. As Pete sang about Tina, there was a catch in his voice and his eyes filled with tears. The television cameras were quick to pick up on this display of emotion; it was plain to everyone in the hall and to the millions watching throughout Europe that this man was singing from the heart.

After strumming the final chord, Pete bowed. For a few seconds there was silence. Then the audience burst into rapturous applause. Everyone got to their feet, screaming and shouting with delight. Kerry Hogan was lost for words. Almost.

'Will yer just listen to the audience?' he enthused. 'I remember, back in the sixties, we had Beatlemania; now it looks as if we've got Wassermania!'

Fully five minutes after Pete had strummed the final chord, the applause showed no sign of abating.

*

After the hubbub had eventually died down, the remaining few songs were performed in an atmosphere of anti-climax. When the final singer had left the stage, Kerry Hogan started to dissect the evening's entertainment as, in most of the capital cities of Europe, small groups of people huddled together in locked rooms to decide how they were going to allocate their votes. The Irishman offered his own assessment:

'The French entry, *Je veux te baiser - la main*,' he said, 'had oodles of Gallic sex-appeal. And what did yer think about that dress the girl was almost wearing? Gravity-defying doesn't come anywhere near to describing it. And the trousers those two lads were poured into? I've not seen the like since poor old PJ Proby split his kecks on stage over thirty years ago.'

The veteran Irishman was now well into his stride: 'And don't get me started on that group from Athens! They call that *dancing*? I've seen more graceful steamrollers. If they were performing in my local taverna, you can bet your last drachma it's not the floor I'd be throwing the plates at! But puttin' all personal bias aside,' he continued, 'the Irish song wasn't at all bad, was it? And that young lady from Germany with the big teeth and the skimpy bikini! Phew! Talk about a thong for Europe!'

Kerry Hogan paused for a moment.

'But the song that really got the crowd going here tonight was, without a shadow of a doubt, *Tina*, the entry from a little country called Slavonicia that it seems hardly anyone has heard of before. To me, the song sounded just like the sort of thing you'd find on the B-side of an auld song from the sixties that never made it anywhere near the charts. But that's probably just me bein' me usual auld curmudgeonly self! And what do you think about that Pete Wasserman, eh? I must admit I'd never heard of him until tonight. But, for my money, he was the star of the show. The audience here in the Lido certainly seemed to think so, too.'

He paused and adjusted his earpiece. 'Well, that's enough from me for now. I'm gettin' the word in me shell-like that the moment of truth has arrived. So let's go straight over to me lovely colleague Sophia, here on the stage of the fabulous Lido in Positaro, to find out how the juries have voted.'

Twenty-eight

Apart from a television monitor and a direct telephone hook-up to the Lido in Positaro, the jury representing each of the participating countries had no means of communication with the outside world. As was the custom in the Eurovision Song Contest, the votes were cast by each country in alphabetical order. Above the stage in the Lido, a huge electronic scoreboard flashed and twinkled, highlighting the constantly changing scores as the votes were declared.

The Austrian, Belgian and Danish juries had all cast their votes - and had caused the first surprise of the evening. Before the start of the contest the French entry had been the hot favourite. Surprisingly, however, despite being awarded the maximum *douze points* by its Swiss neighbour, it had picked up a mere handful of votes from the first six juries. As for the song from Slavonicia, it had attracted a steady smattering of votes and occupied an unremarkable position some two thirds of the way down the league table. Kerry Hogan offered his opinion:

'If I didn't know better, I'd say that there's a conspiracy going on against the French entry! But, as the famous psychiatrist said, just because they're out to get me doesn't mean to say I'm paranoid. Anyway, let's hear again from the gorgeous Sophia.'

'Hello, Helsinki,' said the multilingual beauty. 'Can you hear me?'

'Yes, thank you, Sophia. We are hearing you very well. Here are the votes awarded by the Finnish jury: Austria – eight votes; France – four votes; Germany – three votes; Greece – one vote; Ireland – six votes; Italy – seven votes; Netherlands – five votes; Poland – ten votes; Portugal – two votes; and, finally, the Finnish jury awards twelve votes to ... Slavonicia. And with that, Sophia, we say good night to you from Helsinki.'

'Well, I'm jiggered!' Kerry Hogan could not contain his amazement. 'That Slavonician song is proving to be a bit of a dark horse. It's picking up votes steadily. Now,' he consulted the flashing scoreboard, 'it's crept up into fifth place.'

As the voting continued, the Slavonician entry made further progress: eight votes from Ireland, ten from Poland. There was even a maximum twelve votes from the Italian jury, one of its closest competitors.

'Well, well!' commented Hogan. 'The Poles are in the lead but the song from Slavonicia – and what a real surprise package this entry has turned out to be – is running them a very close second.'

After the Swedish jury had voted, Poland and Slavonicia were dead level. Sophia breathed huskily into her microphone:

'And now let's hear from the final country to vote in this year's contest. Hello, London. May we please have the votes cast by the jury representing the United Kingdom?'

*

The Buddy Holly-style glasses worn by the chairman of the jury in London lent him a scholarly air, an image that he had cultivated assiduously since his days as an undergraduate. It had helped him to progress far beyond the level that his modest abilities would ordinarily have allowed.

After a cock-up which had earned the over-ambitious novice music reporter the biggest bollocking ever handed out by any Fleet Street editor, his career had been on the brink of disintegration before it had barely begun. Almost forty years later, the *brouhaha* over Chas's Merseyside episode at the *Daily Excess* had become part of the folklore of journalism in the watering-holes of Wapping.

Although talent-free, Chas Peacock had been amazingly lucky. At a drinks party to celebrate some long-forgotten scoop by the *Excess*, he had caught the eye of the owner's daughter, a woman in her late twenties of limited educational attainment, even less sexual allure and with a consuming desire to lose her increasingly burdensome virginity.

Her father was equally desperate to get his daughter off the shelf as if she were a bundle of unsold copies of his newspaper. With all the subtlety of one of her father's editorials, she collided with her target, causing him to spill a glass of red wine over her unappetising décolleté. The young man's clumsy attempt to mop up the damage with a handkerchief had served only to immerse him deeper in the mire.

The trainee journalist had risen, with more than a little help from his father-in-law, to his present position as senior music critic for the *Excess*. His professional success, however, was in sharp contrast to his personal life; his marriage to his boss's daughter had remained childless and unsatisfying. During the sexual doldrums which had lasted for years Charles had made every effort to ensure that his occasional departures from the path of righteousness remained undetected.

*

The evening before the Song Contest, Charles was relaxing in front of the television when the phone rang. Irritated at being disturbed in the middle of his favourite programme, he lifted the receiver and snapped: 'Yes? Who is it?'

The male caller, who spoke with a foreign accent, informed him that he knew all about Charles's membership of a certain club south of the river. He intimated that his wife, not to mention her father, would not be best pleased if the public were made aware of his recreational activities. The cost of divorce, added the caller sympathetically, was so high these days, not to mention the damage that such a scandal would do to his reputation. The caller was anxious to respect Charles's right to privacy provided that, the following night, he acted according to the instructions that he was about to receive. He was sure that, as a leading figure in the world of popular music, Charles would experience no difficulty in persuading the other members of his jury to defer to his own extensive musical knowledge.

Charles listened in silence. After conveying his instructions, the caller wished him a pleasant evening and hung up.

'Who was that, Charles?' enquired his wife, who had been in the kitchen.

'No-one, dear,' he lied, trying to keep the tremor out of his voice. 'It was just a cold call from one of those damned double-glazing salesmen.'

'You seemed to be on the phone for quite a long time,' she added. He wondered whether she suspected anything.

'Yes, I find it best to let them talk and I say nothing in response. Eventually they get tired and hang up. I don't think he'll be calling again.'

*

The beautifully modulated tones of the polyglot presenter interrupted Charles's thoughts.

'And now, for the final round of voting, we go to London and the jury of the United Kingdom,' said the talented Sophia. 'As we can see on the scoreboard, the voting is tied for first place. Will the votes that are about to be cast provide us with a winner? Let us find out now from Charles Peacock, the distinguished music critic and Chairman of the United Kingdom jury. Charles, please would you tell us how you have cast your votes?'

'Buono sera, Sophia, cara mio!' he burbled ungrammatically. 'You're looking absolutely sensational this evening - molti bella! Well, Sophia, here are the votes of the United Kingdom jury: Austria – one vote; Denmark – two votes; Greece – three votes; Ireland – four votes; Italy – five votes; Latvia – six votes; Luxembourg – seven votes; Malta – eight votes; Poland - ten votes; and, finally, the United Kingdom jury awards twelve votes to ..' - the word nearly stuck in his throat but he had weighed the odds: after the anonymous phone call he had received, he had no alternative - ' ... Slavonicia!' He almost spat out the word. 'And that concludes the voting by the United Kingdom jury.'

Kerry Hogan nearly dropped his microphone. 'This is absolutely un-be-lievable!' he declared. 'Who would have thought that a country which, let me remind you, scored absolutely no points, zilch, zippo, the last time it entered the Eurovision, has brought off an amazing, astounding victory in this year's contest!'

The television cameras panned to Pete who was standing in the wings. Surrounded by his fellow-competitors who were hiding their disappointment with varying degrees of success, he started to punch the air as he danced a little jig, his paunch wobbling gently.

'Will yer just look at Pete Wasserman!' enthused Kerry Hogan. 'He's going absolutely crazy – anyone would think he'd won the lottery! I'm going to extricate meself from me little cocoon of a studio to try and grab a quick word with him.'

Pete, however, was already back on the stage, his ukulele slung nonchalantly over his shoulder. Pete Wasserman, the king of cool; it was just like when he had been with the Stumblebums. He looked round at his two accompanists and, to rapturous applause, counted them in to a reprise of *Tina*.

*

In her spacious sitting-room, Magdalena Anstruther had eaten her not-quite-in-date microwaveable dinner while watching the Contest. Now that it was over, she stretched out on the sofa, surrounded by dictionaries, thesauri and sundry works of reference, locked in her habitual struggle with the *Telegraph* cryptic crossword. Her husband was in his study, engaged in yet another lengthy telephone conversation. She had the impression that in recent days he had been spending much more time on the phone than usual.

He had just ended the call when his wife called out:

'Douglas?'

'Yes, my dear?'

'I'm having a bit of trouble with three across. The clue is: "gay Installer of eavesdropping device utters expletive" – six letters.'

Sir Douglas looked at his watch and realised with annoyance that he had missed the voting.

'Bugger!' he exclaimed. The study door was open and the sound carried loudly into the lounge.

'Thank you, dear,' replied his wife as she filled in three across, 'but there's no need to shout.'

'Oh, by the way, dear,' he enquired, as casually as he was able, as he came out of his study into the lounge, 'who won the song contest?'

'Well, dear, you know it really is *quite* remarkable. It's that country whose President came round for dinner the other day. You remember – Slavonicia.'

Douglas, with an uncharacteristic display of emotion, clenched his fists and silently mouthed 'yes!' His self-indulgence, however, was only momentary.

'I'm just popping back into the study for a moment,' he said to Magdalena. 'I must make a quick call to congratulate my friend Fyodor.'

'I can't imagine why,' responded his wife. 'He can't possibly be of any use to you. His country isn't even in the European Community, is it?'

If Magdalena Anstruther had not been so engrossed in her crossword, she would have seen on her husband's face, as he turned towards the study door, just the faintest trace of a smile.

*

Pete suddenly realised that he was now a very wealthy man. Half a million pounds would be in his newly-opened account at the Royal Bank of Wales when it opened for business the following Monday morning. 'I just hope the bank don't get robbed like them what I read about on the plane!' he thought to himself.

His mind was racing ahead; the record companies would be falling over themselves to offer him a contract. *Tina* would sell hundreds of thousands of copies, even millions. Maybe, this time, there *would* be a follow-up. Even an album! He owned the copyright to the song, too. There would be loads of money coming in; at last he would be the famous pop star he had told Tina he would be, all those years ago.

Pete looked at Irena who was standing in the wings; tears were cascading down her cheeks.   With difficulty, Pete disentangled himself from the delirious mob of well-wishers and left the stage, brushing aside the thrusting microphones and flashing cameras. He needed to find a phone.

He hoped that International Directory Enquiries would be able to find the number for Tina's sister in Huyton.

Twenty-nine

In his study, Sir Douglas picked up the Edinburgh crystal decanter and poured a small measure of twenty-five year-old Glenfarclas malt into a matching tumbler. The set had been a gift from his wife for his sixtieth birthday. She had bought it in Harrod's sale - a real bargain, less than half the original price. The bubble in the base of one of the glasses was barely visible.

The diplomat added a splash of water, swirled the glass and took a sip. With his free hand he opened a concealed drawer in his bureau and found what he was looking for.

In the black leather ring binder, he looked up the entry marked 'male canine offspring - urine' and studied it for a moment. Smiling, Sir Douglas lifted the scrambler phone from its cradle and dialled the private number of his new friend.

The telephone trilled softly just once before he heard the familiar voice.

'Douglas! My dear friend! How are you?' asked the President. 'I am delighted that you have called. And how is your charming wife?'

'Good evening, Fyodor,' responded the Scot. 'I also am delighted to talk with you again. My wife and I are both very well indeed, thank you. I trust I find you well also? I am calling to offer my most sincere congratulations on your country's splendid victory in the Eurovision Song Contest. I was unable, unfortunately, to watch it myself on the television, but my wife, who is a great devotee of the event, tells me that this year it was unusually dramatic.'

'You are most kind, Douglas,' responded the President. 'It was indeed as you say most dramatic. I was particularly fascinated by the way that the votes were cast. If I did not know better,' he added, 'I should have said that our victory was almost pre-destined.'

Sir Douglas decided to play a straight bat.

'Oh, I am quite sure that Slavonicia's victory was due solely to the excellence of the song and of course,' responded the diplomat smoothly, 'of the singer. I understand that – what is his name? Oh, yes, Pete Wasserman - originates in fact from our own shores. May I express the hope that this will be but the first of many fruitful connections between our two great nations? But forgive me, Fyodor; I am certain that you are very busy with affairs of State and I must not take up any more of your valuable time. Please be assured, however, of the future friendship of my country and, of course, I need hardly add, of my own. I know that the whole of Europe will appreciate the considerable benefits that undoubtedly will accrue. If there is anything I can do to be of assistance at any time in the future, please do not hesitate to let me know.'

The President took Sir Douglas at his word.

'Well, Douglas, as it happens, there *is* something that is of concern to me, but I am reluctant to ask yet another favour of you, especially so soon after your sterling efforts on our nation's behalf. I am already deeply in your debt as a result of the unfortunate misunderstanding involving my daughter. I still do not know how you managed to persuade the head of her college to reconsider the matter.'

Sir Douglas smiled as he recalled his conversation with Octavian Blenkinsop.

The President's voice assumed a graver tone.

'Unfortunately my dear Petrushka has found herself unable to overcome her, er, difficulties and as Slavonicia is not – yet – a member of the European Community, she cannot avail herself of the facilities of your excellent National Health Service. What is more, as I am sure you will be aware, private treatment for such conditions in one of your famous Abbey clinics is extremely expensive. At the risk of seeming selfish, Douglas, should my daughter's situation ever become public knowledge, my government would almost certainly be unable to survive the ensuing scandal. In such an eventuality, a different, dare I say less forward-looking régime might not be so favourably disposed to the idea of Slavonicia facilitating the European Community's desire to establish a military presence in our country.'

President Sonofábic did not labour the point; he was well aware that Sir Douglas fully appreciated the implications for Europe if the proposed UN base in Slavonicia were not to go ahead.

There was a long pause. Sir Douglas sensed that it would be best to wait and let the President make the next move.

President Sonofábic was thinking along similar lines. A moment or two later, the Head of State continued:

'I wonder whether it might be best, all things considered, to continue to satisfy my daughter's needs in this regard.' The President hesitated again. 'There is, however, one further difficulty, Douglas. As I am sure you know, Slavonicia, unfortunately, does not produce the, er, substances to which she has become accustomed. Therefore, as our relations with Colombia are currently somewhat delicate, for reasons that I need not trouble you with, I was wondering whether, perhaps, your own contacts in that part of the world ... ?' The question was left unfinished.

The inflection in the President's voice had changed slightly; Sir Douglas sensed there was something that he was trying to hide. Suddenly the Scot realised what it was and smiled, remembering how delighted the President had been to receive the gift in the brown paper package after their private dinner at his home in London.

The diplomat remained silent; he rather enjoyed this sort of gamesmanship.

After a few seconds, the President coughed. This was, as Sir Douglas had come to realise, a signal that he was about to change the subject. President Sonofábic's tone now seemed much more relaxed.

'But today, Douglas, let us be happy; we have good reason to celebrate! I should like to invite you, my friend, to visit my country - purely in a personal capacity, of course. I am sure, however, that there we shall find an opportunity to discuss many matters of mutual interest. I should deem it a great honour if you would allow me to repay your kindness in assisting my daughter.'

Sir Douglas smiled in appreciation of the President's subtle use of language; it was unclear whether he was alluding to the favour already received or to the one for which he was angling.

Any ambiguity was immediately resolved as President Sonofábic, pursuing his earlier point, suggested: 'Perhaps the Diplomatic Bag ...'

Sir Douglas pursed his lips and pondered for a moment.

'I think that something could possibly be arranged,' he mused, 'but the means you suggest would be, I fear, far too risky. As I am sure you will appreciate, Fyodor, it is essential that our government should not be implicated in this matter in any way. It might be possible, however, to find a suitable person to, er, facilitate your suggestion, but of course, it would be essential that the person concerned be absolutely above suspicion.'

'Do you have someone in mind?' asked the President, eagerly. 'Perhaps one of the junior members of your Royal Family?' he ventured. 'I am given to understand that there are several who are currently experiencing some financial difficulties and might welcome the opportunity to be rewarded handsomely for a task that would require very little effort on their part. My sources tell me that there is one in particular' - he named the person – 'who might be amenable to such a proposition.'

'That is a most interesting idea, Fyodor,' said Lord Anstruther, 'and one that appears to satisfy nearly all of the necessary criteria. However, I can foresee one or two problems. Our popular press, as I think you are aware, is highly intrusive, not to say unscrupulous; there is more than a possibility that such an arrangement would be discovered. If that were the case the consequences would be catastrophic' - Sir Douglas paused for the briefest of moments - 'for both our countries.'

'Hmm, I suppose you have a point there, Douglas,' conceded the President, recalling the time when he had been deported from England following an investigation by one of the Sunday tabloids. He continued, not wanting to let the matter drop: 'Do you have an alternative suggestion?'

Sir Douglas had expected this question.

'May I suggest that you leave this matter with me, Fyodor?' he responded. 'It may take a little while to set things in motion. However, I should be honoured if, in the meantime, you would allow me to send you a small gift. Perhaps you might wish to pass it on to your extremely talented daughter. I gather from my source at St Judas's that her academic ability continues to be exceptional. It would not surprise me in the least if she were to obtain a First.'

Sir Douglas smiled to himself; matters were progressing most satisfactorily. 'Well, goodbye, Fyodor,' he said, 'it has been, as always, a pleasure to talk with you. I am sure that it will not be long before we speak again.'

After putting down the phone Sir Douglas once again opened his black file and read another entry for a few moments. 'Yes,' he murmured, 'that should do very nicely.' The source of his satisfaction was a Third Secretary currently serving in a remote embassy and who had highly unofficial connections with shadowy personages in Colombia. Apart from the young diplomat's supplier and the omniscient Sir Douglas, no-one knew of the junior envoy's predilection for certain substances, a habit which he had acquired at university. Sir Douglas envisaged no difficulty in getting the young man to set up the necessary arrangements between Medellín and Bograd, in return for being allowed to remain on the diplomatic ladder.

At ten o'clock the following morning Sir Douglas had a telephone conversation with the Third Secretary which was brief and to the point.

'That is excellent, my dear young man!' said Sir Douglas in conclusion. 'It is rare that I have the opportunity to speak with someone who combines the energy of youth with the common sense of a much older person, and who has the perspicacity to appreciate implications and take the long view of a situation! And once again, please forgive me.' He looked at his watch; Colombia was in a time zone six hours behind GMT. In Bogotá it was four a.m. He smiled. 'I am so sorry to have disturbed your sleep.'

Thirty

The morning after Pete's unexpected triumph, the hotel receptionist phoned to say that a limousine was waiting to take him to the airport. A private aircraft, she added, was on standby to take him back to England whenever he was ready to leave. There were no further details. Pete supposed that it had all been organised by the Slavonician government.

When he went downstairs, he found Irena in the lobby. She seemed very subdued; it was obvious that the excitement of the previous evening had taken its toll. As Pete got into the car she rushed up to him, burst into tears and threw her arms around his neck.

'You are lovely man, Pete. I going to miss you very big-time. Your Tina, she is very lucky woman.'

As the car sped off Pete was surprised to see, on the bench seat of the limo, a young, attractive blonde. He supposed she must be a groupie.

'Hello, love,' said Pete. 'How did you get in here? Do you want me autograph or something?'

'No, Pete,' replied the blonde, huskily. 'I'm looking for *much* more than that.'

*

The editor of the *Planet*, the *Daily Excess*'s deadliest rival in the never-ending newspaper circulation war, had come to a decision: no expense would be spared to secure an exclusive interview with the man whose song had taken Europe by storm.

'He's really hot news, is this Wasserman chap,' he emphasised at the daily briefing of section heads. 'It's just the sort of story our readers will go for: "middle-aged drunken slob finds fame and fortune".'

An earnest-looking young woman was scribbling down what he had said.

'For Christ's sake don't use that as a headline!' he bellowed. 'I'm sure you'll be able to come up with something a bit more imaginative to hook the great British public with.'

The tabloid's editor had chartered a Lear jet and despatched a keen young reporter to bring the conquering hero back to the UK. The instructions given to the leggy blonde allowed no room for misunderstanding: she was to do whatever was necessary to get Pete to talk. Her career prospects at the *Planet,* the editor had told her, would depend on the outcome of this mission. As she took Pete by the arm, she reflected that her degree in Ethics and Moral Philosophy had not exactly been an ideal preparation for the task that now lay before her.

A long line of passengers waiting impatiently to check in glared at Pete and the blonde as they walked towards the Departure gates. Two *carabinieri* smiled and saluted as they passed. No attempt was made to check their identity or their progress as Pete and the blonde made their way towards a remote door marked 'VIP'. Pete hesitated and turned to the young woman:

'Don't I need a ticket or somethin'? And what about me bags?' he asked.

'Don't worry about any of that, Pete,' she said, airily. 'Everything's been taken care of. No customs, no red tape, no problems. My boss has friends in high places. By the way,' she smiled, holding out a beautifully manicured hand, 'my name's Davina.'

When they had boarded the plane, Pete looked around him.

'Where are the other passengers, then?' he asked.

The young woman smiled. 'There *are* no other passengers, Pete; it'll be just you and me. Oh, and the pilot, too, of course!' she laughed. 'We'll have a lovely, comfy few hours, up in the air, all on our own, miles high … ' - she lingered over the phrase - ' There'll be plenty of time for us to get better acquainted over a bottle or two of bubbly.'

The excitement and tensions of the past few months had finally caught up with Pete. After one glass of champagne, and much to the annoyance of his travelling companion, he closed his eyes and slept for the duration of the flight.

*

The dying whine of the engines, as the plane came to a halt at its stand, was replaced by another, shriller sound. Through a window Pete could see hundreds of fans waiting to welcome him home.

As he came down the steps of the plane, he was greeted again by cameras flashing and microphones being thrust under his nose. Davina steered him through the throng, whisking him past smiling customs officials. None of them was going to risk the wrath of the fans by subjecting him or his luggage to the indignity of being searched.

Suddenly he saw Tina. She was standing alone, at the back of the crowd, the only person there who was not trying to shake his hand or kiss him. Pete pushed his way towards her. They looked at one another awkwardly for a moment, like teenagers unsure how to say goodbye after a first date.

'I've missed you,' he said.

'Me too,' she replied. 'Where are you going to be staying?'

'I dunno,' he replied. 'I haven't really thought about it.'

'You haven't changed, have you? You're still hopeless,' she said, her voice a mixture of exasperation and affection. 'I hated you, you know, that night when you came home drunk and were sick on the carpet. I could have killed you!'

Pete looked at her, not knowing what to do or say. Without warning Tina slapped his face.

'I deserved that,' said Pete, quietly.

Tina threw her arms around him again. 'You'd better come back with me,' she said. 'I'm staying with my sister Maureen. '

'I'd like that, Tina,' said Pete. 'I'd like that very much.'

*

The next morning, as Pete and Tina were having breakfast, Maureen made it clear that she wasn't happy about his sudden reappearance into her sister's life.

'Our Tina's had a tough time,' she said tersely. 'I don't want her to get hurt again. I just want her to be happy.'

'It's alright, Maureen,' said Tina, 'I know what I'm doing.' She started to clear away the breakfast things.

Pete followed her into the kitchen.

'Don't mind my sister,' she said. 'She's only looking out for me.'

Tina paused for a moment. 'Listen, I've had an idea. Why don't we go away, just the two of us, just to get away from everything?'

'Where d'yer wanna go?'

'How about the Metropole in Southport, just for a few days, so's we can decide what we're going to do? We tried to go there once, do you remember, before we got married, but you said the bar was closed. I've always fancied staying there.'

'Sounds great,' agreed Pete. 'Yer mean like a second honeymoon, sort of thing?'

'Yeh, the first one wasn't much cop, was it?' she smiled ruefully. 'You remember that awful boarding house, don't you?'

'How could I forget it? Tell you what, will you book it, Tina? You know I'm no good at that sort of thing.'

*

'Southport must be the only seaside resort in the country where you have to go on a day trip to see the sea!' laughed Tina as they walked along the promenade. They spent the next couple of days just walking around the town, hand in hand, without a care in the world.

Pete remembered a pub he had been to a few times when he was a lad. The Frog and Dartboard was just off Lord Street, he told her.

'That's a funny name for a pub!' she chuckled.

'Yeah, I know, but they do a great pie and chips,' he said enthusiastically. 'D'yer fancy it?'

'Yeah, why not?' said Tina. 'Yer can't beat the simple things in life.'

They found, to their disappointment, that the place had been renamed and was now part of a national chain of gastropubs. There was no mention on the menu of pie and chips.

Thirty-one

For several days Pete's success in the Eurovision had been splashed all over the tabloids. Many of them had produced in-depth articles about the singer, charting his rise from obscurity to international celebrity. The *Custodian* sought to add an intellectual dimension to this rags-to-riches story by devoting a leading article to Pete, enthusing polysyllabically about his self-deprecating humour and his uncanny appreciation of the *zeitgeist*. Not to be outdone, the *Epoch* weighed in with a lengthy piece by its music editor who had detected in Pete's performance of *Tina* the understated influence of early Appalachian folk music with an admixture of Victorian music hall comedy.

When they got back to Tina's sister's house, Maureen told Pete that there had been dozens of messages from agents who were anxious to look after his interests. The calls went unanswered; the only thing on Pete's mind was Tina.

*

A few days later Pete went with Tina on a shopping expedition in the city centre. As they passed an estate agent's window Tina paused to have a look. Excitedly she grabbed Pete's arm.

'Look, Pete! There's a house for sale in Menlove Avenue! I've always wanted to live there, ever since I was a little girl. Let's go in and ask about it.'

The young man in the agency gave Tina a brochure describing the property. Excitedly, she read it aloud to Pete:

'We are delighted to have received exclusive instructions from the vendor to offer an extremely rare opportunity to acquire this highly desirable, mature, four-bedroom residence in a much sought-after area. The property offers the exceptional amenity of three reception rooms as well as a conveniently-sized morning room. There is also a downstairs cloakroom.' Tina looked at Pete to see his reaction. She continued: 'The large, well-stocked gardens, laid mainly to lawn and boasting a wide variety of flowering trees and shrubs, afford complete privacy and total seclusion from neighbouring properties.'

As a further inducement there was, the brochure proclaimed, considerable scope for the discerning purchaser with imagination and vision to develop to contemporary standards the outstanding potential of this remarkable family dwelling.

'Oh, Pete,' exclaimed Tina. 'It sounds perfect! We've gorra go and see it!'

The house on Menlove Avenue was indeed remarkable; the sheet describing the property had made full use of the estate agent's considerable stock of hyperbole and euphemisms in his attempt to render the house an attractive proposition to prospective purchasers.

When they visited the property the following day, Tina discovered that 'mature' meant decrepit, 'conveniently-sized' signified poky, and that 'outstanding potential' indicated that the building needed a fortune spending on it.

Tina's ambition to live in Menlove Avenue far outweighed the depressing evidence of her own eyes. Tina had set her heart on living there and such a minor consideration as money, especially now that Pete was going to be mega-rich, was not going to get in the way.

The agent sensed that he was close to getting the property off his books. Because of its condition it had been a real bugger to shift. Perhaps, he thought, if he fed the couple a little more background information it might clinch the deal.

'As you have seen, madam, the house has a downstairs cloakroom. That, I understand, is why it's called *Toulouse*,' he said, smiling. 'The vendor is a retired French teacher with a sense of humour.'

'We never even had *one* loo in our house in Toxteth!' said Pete. Tina carried on: 'Yeah, and it's got *three* reception rooms! Just think, Pete! We could have receptions in the morning and in the afternoon. And we could have another one in the evening! We *can* buy it, can't we, Pete? Please say we can!'

'You can have anythin' you want, darlin',' said Pete. Tina hugged him.

As Tina and Pete were leaving the house, she turned to the young man who had been showing them round the property:

'By the way, how much is it?'

*

Percy Coggins, the manager of the Liverpool City Centre branch of the Royal Bank of Wales, fitted perfectly the stereotypical image of his profession. In his late fifties, short, balding and running to fat, he bore more than a passing resemblance to Captain Mainwaring from *Dad's Army*. He preferred to remain within the sanctuary of his office, discreetly hidden away from the public whom he regarded as an inconvenience. Mr Coggins spent his working days typing information into his computer, his activity interrupted only by the mid-morning ritual of a cup of coffee with two ginger nut biscuits and, at less regular intervals, a telephone call from his superiors at Regional Head Office.

Today, however, was to provide an exception to Mr Coggins's routine. Just as he was dunking the first of his biscuits into his bone china cup – a delicate manoeuvre which called for precise calculation of exactly how long to immerse the biscuit without a piece breaking off and falling in – there was an urgent knock on his door. Without waiting for an invitation to enter, a junior member of staff rushed in and informed him excitedly that Pete Wasserman, the winner of the Eurovision Song Contest, was waiting outside.

The manager's normally calm demeanour vanished; it was not generally known that Percy Coggins was a huge fan of the Contest and that each year at his large, comfortable home in Crosby he hosted for his exclusively male social circle a grand Eurovision party. Pete Wasserman was, in his eyes, an heroic figure, living proof of what he, Percy Coggins, might have achieved had his life taken a different course.

Distracted from his biscuit-dunking, Mr. Coggins failed to react with sufficient speed to prevent a large piece of ginger nut from breaking away from the mother biscuit and plopping into the cup, almost splashing his shirt. The manager however was unconcerned by this near miss; he stood up, carefully adjusted the knot on his tie and emerged with uncharacteristic speed from his office. He greeted Pete and Tina with a huge smile and a firm handshake.

'May I offer my congratulations, Mr Wasserman, to the many that I am sure you have already received?' The manager ignored Tina. 'May I say how grateful we are that you have favoured us with your custom.'

Pete did not inform him of the ill-disguised contempt with which he had been treated by one of the cashiers on the only previous occasion that he had set foot in the same branch of this eminent financial institution.

'How may we be of service to you, Mr Wasserman?' asked Mr Coggins, exuding more oil than the Exxon Valdes. He could not do enough for Pete; having ushered the couple back into his office, he listened while Pete and Tina explained about the house on Menlove Avenue that they wanted to buy. The manager assured them that the bank would be delighted to advance as much money as they desired.

'The bank's normal policy is to require the borrower to put down a deposit of ten per cent of the purchase price. In your case, this would amount to … '

When he stated the sum, Pete's mouth fell open in horror. The manager, noticing his reaction, was quick to reassure him.

'However in these, er, exceptional circumstances I am sure that I shall be able to use my influence, which I flatter myself in saying is not inconsiderable, to persuade Head Office to advance you the full purchase price, plus a further sum for the improvements that I am sure you will undoubtedly wish to make to the property. We understand, naturally, that you would not wish to draw on the considerable sum that you have on deposit with us. That in itself will, I am sure, be acceptable as collateral for the loan. At the Royal Bank of Wales we pride ourselves on always having the best interests of our customers at heart.'

Mr Coggins neglected to mention that the bank would be making considerably more interest on the money that Pete had on deposit than it would be giving to him. He continued:

'In your particular case, I am of the opinion that a 150% mortgage would be perfectly in order. I hope that will be sufficient for your requirements? Yes? Good! So, if you would be kindly sign these forms here … and here … and again, just here. Thank you very much, Mr Wasserman. Excellent!' The manager took the completed forms and placed them in one of the drawers of his desk.

'Now, Mr Wasserman, perhaps I can interest you in our very special credit card offer that we have available at the moment for a limited period only.' Mr. Coggins proceeded to explain the myriad advantages of the bank's plastic product. 'Naturally, for a man in your position there would be no question of us having to make the usual credit checks. And we should not dream of insulting you by asking you to provide personal references. If you have not had a credit card before, you will find it extremely convenient, not to say liberating. For example you won't need to carry any cash on you.' The bank manager hazarded a joke. 'Just like the Royal Family! Oh yes,' he added as an afterthought, 'we should be prepared to extend the same facility to Mrs Wasserman.'

Thirty-two

Pete and Tina had needed no further encouragement to act on the bank manager's invitation. Their new house was unoccupied and although it needed a lot of work doing on it, they decided to move in as soon as possible. After handing in her notice at Tesco Tina divided her time over the next few months between shopping expeditions as far afield as Manchester and London, and supervising the extensive alterations she had planned.

Pete was quite content to leave his wife to buy everything she thought they needed. The only item that he quite fancied was an electronic piano that recorded songs while you were playing them. The instrument cost a couple of thousand but that was chickenfeed, he told himself, compared with what he would be raking in from now on. It would pay for itself in no time flat, especially when he released *Tina*.

One morning, with her new plastic companion, Tina took a taxi to go shopping in Wilmslow. She guessed that the fare would only be about fifty quid, each way. She had read that Wilmslow was where lots of famous footballers lived; it would be exciting, she thought, if she bumped into one of them.

In one of the glossy magazines at the hairdresser's she had also seen a feature about the opening of a new branch of an upmarket chain of stores specialising in kitchen gadgets. Two hours later, she emerged from Lochside Plastics with four bulging carrier bags bearing the store's garish logo. Tina could not imagine how generations of housewives had survived without such culinary essentials as an electric kiwi peeler, a stainless steel banana hanger or a thermometer for testing the temperature of baked potatoes.

Gone, also, were the days of standing in the rain at the bus stop, getting splashed by passing cars. Tina, having obtained a provisional driving licence, had wasted no time in going to an upmarket car dealer and putting down a deposit on a top of the range coupé. She had shown not the slightest interest in the salesman's patter about the vehicle's technical specification; what she had been unable to resist was the pink coachwork.

*

One morning while Tina was out shopping, Pete took a break from watching daytime TV. He wandered into the recently installed luxury kitchen to make himself a drink. He was slowly getting the hang of the shiny Italian coffee machine with an unpronounceable name.

Absorbed in the device's various switches, knobs and levers, Pete did not hear the BMW as it glided to a halt outside the house. A few moments later the doorbell rang to the chimes of the first few bars of *Tina*.

'Hello, Pete!' exclaimed the young man standing on the doorstep.

Pete looked blankly at his visitor.

'You won't remember me, I don't suppose? I was just a very young kid back then. I'm Jimmy, Jimmy Grant. You knew my father, Don Grant?' he continued. 'He was your manager for a while back in the early sixties when you were with that band, what was it called? Oh, yeah, that's it, the Stumblebums.'

He looked round Pete's living room and whistled appreciatively. 'It certainly looks like you've done OK for yourself since then!'

'Er, yeah, what can I do for you, like?' he asked, politely.

'Well, Pete,' said his visitor, 'It's really more about what *I* can do for *you*. Perhaps if I could come inside for a moment we could have a little chat and I could explain things in a bit more detail.'

*

As Jimmy Grant sipped his cappuccino, his tone became more serious. He leaned forward in his armchair.

'You know, Pete, my dad was always telling me that you were the only one in that group who had any real musical talent. And that's why I'm here now.'

His voice became sombre. 'Dad died recently and I've been going through his papers and stuff. I'd been working with him in the agency for a few years, learning the ropes, and now it's just me running the business. Anyway, I came across your name and of course, in view of your recent success, I thought it would be a good idea to get in touch. I just wanted to make sure that you weren't being taken for a ride by some shark of an agent. You have to be very careful these days, there's a lot them about.'

Jimmy Grant put down his cup and smiled at Pete.

'I want to take your career to the next level; you know, build on your Eurovision success. I reckon, with the right management, you could really go places. Today, Europe; tomorrow, who knows where? I've done OK for myself, too, as you can see.'

He gestured expansively through the lounge window at the BMW. It slipped his mind to inform Pete that the car had been hired for the day.

'If you're interested,' Grant continued, 'I could fix you up with a recording contract with one of the big boys. I'm pretty sure that I could get you some appearances on TV, too. I've heard that Parkinson is really keen to have you on his show. And what do you think about this, Pete? My contacts in London have said they may be interested in producing a musical based on your life. You could really make a mint! And the best thing of all is that you won't need to worry about organising anything; I'll take care of all that.' Pete didn't detect Jimmy Grant's switch of tense from the conditional to the future.

Since the night of the Song Contest, Pete hadn't spent much time thinking about what he was going to do. What Jimmy Grant was proposing sounded impressive; he particularly liked the idea of not having to organise anything himself.

When the impresario held out his pen and said 'Just sign here,' Pete didn't hesitate.

Thirty-three

'Good morning,' said the posh-sounding young voice on the phone. 'I wonder if it would be possible to speak with Mr Peter Wasserman?'

'That's me, pal,' yawned Pete who had just woken up. The one o'clock news was starting on the television which he had forgotten to turn off the night before. 'Who's this?'

'My name's Matthew Whitelaw, Mr Wasserman. I'm speaking on behalf of the Union. We'd like ...'

'Sorry, pal,' interrupted Pete, 'I don't belong to no union. Mind you,' he added, trying to be helpful, 'me dad always voted Labour.'

'No, Mr Wasserman,' laughed the young man. 'The reason for my call has nothing to do with politics but, now that you mention it, many of our members have indeed gone on to make a career in the House.'

Pete was sympathetic. 'I bet it must be a real drag for them, having to stay at home all day, doing the housework and stuff. Couldn't they get a proper job, like?'

The caller laughed loudly. 'I'd been told that you have a great sense of humour, Mr Wasserman. Now I can hear for myself just how true that is. But let me tell you the reason why I'm calling you today. The Union to which I was referring is in fact the University of Oxford debating society. Following your recent success in the Eurovision Song Contest, you have become quite a celebrity and we should consider it a great honour if you would agree to take part in one of our forthcoming debates. We wonder whether you would be willing to speak in favour of the motion that "The Eurovision Song Contest is not an anachronism"?'

'Well,' said Pete. 'I was certainly knackered afterwards, all right.'

Matthew Whitelaw laughed again. 'You are certainly quite a wag, Mr Wasserman! I'm sure you'll be a big hit with our members. Naturally, we shall be more than happy to cover all your expenses and we shall be delighted to offer you accommodation in one of our most prestigious colleges, St. Judas's. Oh, yes,' continued the President of the Oxford Union. 'There's just one further thing. I nearly forgot to mention it. It's black tie, of course.'

Pete accepted the invitation; he wasn't sure whether, after forty years or so, he still had the black tie he had bought to wear for his parents' funeral.

*

Since the opening of its present building in the late nineteenth century, the Oxford Union had invited a wide variety of guest speakers from all over the world. Scientists, actors, musicians and sports personalities were among those who had ventured into the bear pit of its debating chamber. It was here that future Prime Ministers, many of them educated at the nation's most prestigious schools, had honed their public speaking skills, leaning casually against the dispatch box and surviving on their wits in a manner that they would seek to emulate later at Westminster. It was into this intimidating atmosphere that Pete Wasserman innocently stepped, armed only with his ukulele which, since his victory, he always carried with him for luck.

Pete was dressed for the occasion in his best jeans and a white, short-sleeved shirt. He had not forgotten what the President had said just before the end of their conversation: around his neck he wore a black string tie. The President of the Oxford Union looked with raised eyebrows at his fellow officials, who shrugged helplessly at this unprecedented breach of etiquette.

As the Eurovision Song Contest winner entered the chamber, the student members of the Union rendered their instantaneous verdict on Pete's sartorial sense; they greeted his literal interpretation of the dress code with a roar of approval. It was immediately evident to all that his reputation as a wag, noted by the President of the Union and advertised prior to the debate, was fully deserved. The crowd was on his side, even before he had uttered a word.

The debate began with a long, boring speech from the Secretary of State for the Arts who, in a thinly veiled attack on the Song Contest, deplored the depths to which contemporary culture had sunk. In the Cabinet reshuffle the previous week, he had been promoted from his junior post at the Department of Agriculture and Fisheries as a reward for heading off another cod war. Unfortunately, in the brief period since his elevation, the Minister had had little opportunity to extend his cultural hinterland. His views were tediously conventional; he had evidently briefed himself by reading the *Excess*.

There were a few isolated cries of 'hear, hear' from those members of the audience who had managed to remain awake during his twenty-minute address. Encouraged by their support the Minister trawled the murky depths of his memory and dredged up a line from *Twelfth Night*. Learnt at his prep school several decades previously, this snippet from Shakespeare had not been called into active service since.

The Secretary of State for the Arts stood erect, his left arm outstretched in what he imagined to be a dramatic pose. His gaze swept the room, as he recalled his English master having done at Cheambury. Ponderously, he intoned: 'If music be the food of love ...'

Pete's reading seldom extended further than the headlines in the tabloids and the occasional article in the musical press. His knowledge of song lyrics from the sixties was, however, encyclopaedic. When the Minister paused, Pete thought that he had forgotten the rest of the line. In a spirit of helpfulness, he blurted out: 'prepare for indigestion'.

The audience erupted into gales of laughter. The students in the debating chamber were far too young to know that Pete's apparently original *bon mot* came from the title of an old album by a sixties group which went by the name of Dave Dee, Dozy, Beaky, Mick and Titch. Pete's unwitting witticism transformed him instantly into a cult hero.

The Minister, deflated, collapsed onto his seat. When the cheering had finally subsided, Pete got to his feet. He didn't have a clue about what he was going to say. He looked round the chamber at the smiling faces of the students. He cleared his throat nervously. A member of the audience shouted out: 'Give us a song, Pete!'

Pete stopped to consider this request. It wasn't unreasonable, he thought; music was, after all, what he understood best. He picked up his ukulele and started to strum the opening chords to *Tina*. He had sung only three words when the entire audience stood as one and joined in. Pete didn't have to continue. Their response indicated beyond doubt that the Eurovision Song Contest was indeed not an anachronism. The voting that followed was a mere formality.

Pete's unintentional triumph made the front page in several of the following day's national newspapers. Even the *Nonpartisan,* whose policy was to maintain a lofty indifference towards what it considered to be ephemeral popular concerns, devoted an editorial to Pete, applauding his elevation to the Pantheon of popular culture, where he had now joined the select few – it referred to him in the same sentence as Elvis and Kylie - who could be identified merely by the mention of their forename.

The tabloids were equally enthusiastic. 'Pete's neat feat!' was the headline in the *Planet*. There was even an article in the newspaper's Scottish edition proposing that a campaign be launched for Pete to stand as a candidate for the soon-to-be-vacant position of Rector of Glasgow University.

Thirty-four

While the builders were knocking things down then putting things up, the house on Menlove Avenue looked like a bomb site. The renovation work on the house and garden took almost a year to complete, but the couple were happy as Tina's dream home took shape.

Once the work was completed, however, they began to realise that it was not just the house that had changed. Tina no longer had anything worthwhile to do to occupy her days; she missed her workmates at the supermarket. They'd had some good laughs together. Now she felt almost lonely. She tried to fill her time with messing about in the garden, shopping for things she knew she didn't need and going to the gym.

Pete, meanwhile, spent his time trying without success to write a follow-up to *Tina*, punctuating his efforts with lunches in the pub with his mates from the old days. He was making a genuine effort, however, not to let his drinking get out of hand.

Their otherwise parallel lives intersected only in the evenings. Tina, by her own admission, had never been a great cook but that didn't matter to Pete; he was perfectly happy to eat microwave-ready meals from Marks and Spencer as they sat, each with a tray on their knees, watching TV or DVDs before going to bed and immediately falling asleep.

Each of them came to realise that things were not working out, but neither wanted to be the first to talk about it.

*

Early one evening, Pete found an old takeaway menu from the Star of Bengal, still in business after all these years. It was now offering a free delivery service for customers living within a one-mile radius of the restaurant. For deliveries to more remote addresses, he read, there was a £2 per mile supplementary charge. He picked up the phone and ordered a vindaloo for himself and a chicken korma for Tina.

Half an hour later, the doorbell rang. Cradled in the arms of Mr Mukherjee, the proprietor of the Star of Bengal, was a large cardboard box piled high with an extensive selection of the culinary masterpieces of his head chef. Mr Mukherjee had insisted on delivering the food personally. Furthermore, he refused to accept any payment; he was already relishing the prospect of being able to boast to his friends about his most famous customer. Perhaps an advertisement in the *Echo* would not be a bad idea, too, he thought to himself.

For the best part of an hour Pete ploughed through the contents of the foil containers while Tina picked at her chicken korma. As Pete pushed away the box containing the remnants of his vindaloo, he belched contentedly. Tina suddenly reached for the remote and turned off the TV. Pete looked at her questioningly.

'Let's be honest, Pete,' she said, her eyes filling with tears. 'It's just not working, is it?'

Pete felt a sense of relief; he had been thinking the same thing but hadn't dared to say anything to Tina for fear of upsetting her again.

'You're right, love. Thanks for tryin'. I really thought we could go back to how it used to be when we was both kids, but ...' The sentence remained unfinished. He looked at Tina, smiling sadly. 'No 'ard feelin's, then?'

'Course not, Pete,' she smiled. 'We'll always be best friends.' Her face brightened. 'Look, I'll sort out getting this place sold. With everything we've spent on it, we may even make a bit of money! In the meantime, we can both stay here, can't we – just as friends?'

*

The next day, over a ploughman's lunch, Pete was chatting with a pal from the old days when he had been working as an assistant caretaker at LIPA.

'You must be loaded, mate, with all the dosh you've made from that song contest,' reckoned his friend. 'You shouldn't just leave all your money in the bank. When you take inflation into account, it's just losing its value. What you need,' he suggested, 'is a financial adviser. I can put you on to someone who knows about investments and all that sort of thing. Fife Doberman, his name is. He's a Yank. His dad was a Jock. He's married to my cousin's uncle. Sound as a pound, he is. Well, sound as a dollar, anyway. Why don't you have a chat with him?'

*

When Pete turned up at the bank a few days later, Percy Coggins's tranquillity was disturbed for a second time by another urgent knock on the door of his office. When he was informed of the reason for Pete's visit the shock caused him to drop an entire ginger nut into his cup of coffee and splash his clean white shirt with Gold Blend. These things didn't happen in the TV adverts, thought Mr Coggins as he dabbed furiously at his chest. He succeeded only in making the stain worse. What filled him with dread, however, was the prospect of having to inform his superior at Regional Head Office that his most prestigious client had decided to take all his money out of his account - almost five hundred thousand pounds.

*

'In today's stock market, Mr Wasserman,' Fife Doberman assured Pete, 'technology is the only place to be for the smart investor. You can see it for yourself - everyone is rushing to buy computers, laptops, software, games and so on. They're just flying off the shelves. The market is extremely buoyant at the present time and, from my experience, I believe it's going to rise even higher. In fact, there's no telling how high it will go. We really shouldn't delay; the sooner I invest you in the market, the sooner your capital will start working for you. The way things are going, I shouldn't be surprised if you get a return of at least fifteen, no, make that twenty per cent each year. And there's hardly any paperwork - there's just one form for you to sign. I'll take care of everything else.'

The American held out a sheet of paper to Pete and smiled reassuringly. 'Just sign here - and here - and here. Thank you, that's perfect. Here's your copy. You can relax now, Mr Wasserman; just leave everything to me. Oh yes, I nearly forgot! I just need you to let me have the money. A cheque will do just fine.' Doberman hesitated for a moment. 'Could you make it out to cash?'

In return for a commission of only fifteen percent, which he assured Pete was a specially discounted rate for the fortunate few whom he described as his blue chip clients, Fife Doberman told Pete that he had invested the money in the Comet Universal New Technology fund which for the past few months, he informed him, had been outperforming all the others in its sector of the stock market. Pete was impressed; he liked the sound of 'outperforming.'

*

Pete was feeling quite pleased with himself. Having finally mastered the coffee machine he was sipping a double espresso one morning as he sprawled on the white leather sofa in front of the television. Tina, on a matching recliner chair, put down her cappuccino and pressed a button to electronically adjust the seat. They sat in companionable silence, like two friends just house-sitting for someone else.

During the midday bulletin, the newsreader's voice suddenly wavered in mid-item. Her left hand fiddled with her almost invisible earpiece to check that what she was hearing was correct. She coughed and turned very pale. Pete wondered whether the colour balance on the TV needed seeing to.

'We're just getting some breaking news from the London Stock Exchange. In the last hour the index of leading shares, the Footsie 100, has plunged over a thousand points, wiping more than fifty billion pounds off the value of the top one hundred companies in the UK. Initial reports seem to suggest that this dramatic fall is due to a sudden loss of investor confidence in the technology sector, caused apparently by serious overproduction of semiconductors by tiger economies in the Pacific Rim. According to City analysts, this downturn is unprecedented in modern times and is on a scale not witnessed since the Wall Street crash of 1929. We'll bring you further updates as we receive them.'

Tina looked at Pete. Her eyes were already filling with tears.

'Didn't that man, whatsisname, Doberman, invest all our money in technology stocks, Pete?'

'Never mind, love,' said her husband. 'It'll all be OK. There's nutten' ter worry about; we'll be fine.' An idea occurred to him. 'Tell yer what. I'll give him a bell, if yer like.'

Pete tried Doberman's mobile six times. Each time he heard the same recorded message: 'Sorry, the number you have dialled is unobtainable.'

Pete was not perturbed. 'Anyway,' he sought to reassure Tina, 'we've got the royalty money comin' in from the sales of *Tina*. And Jimmy Grant is gonna be ringin' me later this mornin' about the recordin' contract and the musical.'

The expected phone call from Don Grant's son didn't come that morning. Nor did they heard anything that afternoon. Tina started to panic.

'You know that contract you signed with him? Where's your copy?'

Pete looked for the piece of paper he had signed and eventually found it under a pile of CDs and magazines. Tina grabbed the sheet out of his hand and read it in silence. Her face turned white.

'You didn't look at it before you signed it, did you?' she whispered.

At the bottom of the document was a single sentence in very small print. It read: "95% of all royalties accruing from the work of Peter Wasserman are to be paid directly to James Grant in whom, in consideration of his professional services, sole copyright is hereby vested."

Tina looked at Pete, ashen-faced.

'Oh! Pete!' she sobbed, 'it's my fault, all the money I've spent.'

'No, Tina, love, you're not to blame for anything. We was both chasin' a dream. It wasn't meant to be, but we 'ad to try! Even if we lose everything, we won't be any worse off than we ever was. It'll be alright, I promise!'

The silence was broken by the cheerful whistle of the postman as he pushed the day's mail through the letterbox.

The credit card bills were starting to come in.

Thirty-five

'No expense has been spared,' stated the estate agent's blurb in the glossy *Merseyside Life*, 'on this dream home, which has been completely updated to the very highest specifications. Do not miss the opportunity to view!'

The house on Menlove Avenue had been attracting considerable interest. Unfortunately, none of the dozens of people who claimed to be interested in buying the property followed up their visit with a firm offer.

'All fur coat and no knickers, that lot,' said Pete after the umpteenth frivolous enquirer had tramped through their house. 'They're just a load of nosey buggers.' It was the first time Tina had seen him angry.

'We can't drop the price, neither, Pete,' sobbed Tina. 'Even at the price we're asking we're not going to make a penny on the house. How are we going to pay for everything?'

*

Mr Coggins fully appreciated the difficult circumstances in which Mr and Mrs Wasserman currently found themselves but he regretted to have to inform them that so far no payments had been made to reduce the amount owing to the bank. The interest charges, too, were causing the amount outstanding to increase significantly each week. Perhaps, Mr Coggins wondered politely, Mr and Wasserman might be able to find time to drop in to the branch for an informal chat, to see if the bank could be of assistance.

Mr Coggins received no reply. A further, more strongly-worded letter was sent from Regional Head Office, with the same result. A final letter, this time from National Head Office threatening legal action to recover the money due to the bank, also remained unanswered.

*

Pete and Tina were fast asleep in their separate bedrooms when the doorbell rang. Pete grunted and turned over, pulling the quilt over his head to try to shut out the noise. The bell kept ringing. Very reluctantly, his head emerged from beneath the quilt and he opened one eye to look at the clock radio on the bedside table. The red LED display showed seven fifty-nine. It was still pitch black. 'Fuckin' hell!' he muttered. The doorbell kept ringing. He jabbed randomly at the buttons and heard the pips for the news.

'It's eight o'clock; here are the news headlines,' said the announcer. 'Later this morning, the Prime Minister will be holding talks with …'

Pete's brain gradually focused. Who the hell, he wondered, could be ringing his doorbell at this time of day? He stumbled out of bed, pulled on his tracksuit bottoms and the sweatshirt he had worn the previous day.

'Stay where you are, Tina,' he shouted from outside her bedroom door. 'I'll see who it is.' Hanging onto the banister, he staggered downstairs.

The doorbell continued to ring with increasing urgency.

'OK, OK, I'm comin', for Christ's sake!' he shouted. When he opened the door, he was confronted by three solid-looking men in dark suits.

'Mr Peter Wasserman?' said one. The question was rhetorical. The man took out an official-looking document from his pocket and read it aloud in a monotone:

'Pursuant to a County Court Judgment made against you in favour of the Royal Bank of Wales and others, we are hereby empowered to distrain upon your property goods and chattels equating to the value of the monies owed to the aforementioned creditors. In this instance, goods and chattels to the value of' - he looked briefly at the document for confirmation - 'four hundred and seventy-seven thousand, eight hundred and forty-six pounds' - the man looked at Pete - 'and sixty-two pence.'

The men brushed past Pete and began, in silence, to remove all of his and Tina's possessions. He watched, impotently, as they carried out of the house to a waiting van virtually everything he and Tina had bought.

'Car keys, please,' said the chief bailiff, holding out a hand.

Pete, in shock, handed over the keys to Tina's sports car and his own Range Rover which had never left the driveway since the day he had had it delivered.

Apart from their two beds and duvets, a kettle and a can opener, they were left with nothing. The only other items that the men had not taken away were Pete's Clavinova, a battered old guitar and his precious ukulele: the rules under which bailiffs carried out their joyless work specified that they were not permitted to deprive a person of the tools of their trade.

The bank, the bailiffs further informed Pete, had obtained an eviction order against him; in one week's time, Pete and Tina would be out on the street. The only thing Pete had left was his music.

Tina and Pete stood in silence in the empty house.

'It *is* all my fault, Pete,' said Tina. 'I'm so, so sorry.' Her face brightened momentarily. 'Look, I've got £300 in my Post Office account. You can have that.'

'Hey, come on, Tina,' said Pete. 'We've been through it all before. It's *not* your fault. I think you should go back to Huyton and stay with your sister until all this blows over. I don't want you stayin' 'ere, in this 'ouse, if things turn nasty! No arguments, Tina; I mean it!'

Tina didn't argue. 'But you will be alright, won't you, Pete?' she asked anxiously.

'Course I will, you know me! I'll phone you every week. That's a promise. Now you'd better get goin', alright?'

Tina packed her suitcase. Pete walked her slowly to the bus stop. A bus arrived almost straightaway. As it pulled away, she blew him a kiss through the window.

*

Pete, virtually penniless, didn't have a clue about what he was going to do next. He decided to go down to LIPA to see if he could have his old job back, but drew a blank.

As he was walking away dejectedly Pete heard someone call out his name. At first he didn't recognise the man who was limping along with the aid of a stick. Then he realised who it was: Dean, one of his old bandmates from the Stumblebums.

'Hey! How're you doin', la?' he asked Pete. 'I saw you on the Eurovision. You was fantastic! Yer must be minted now!'

Over a coffee – Dean wasn't allowed to drink alcohol, he told Pete, because of his gout - he talked about his life since the Stumblebums had broken up. His window cleaning enterprise had been a big success, especially after Jimmy, with whom he had set it up, had got bored with it and had sold him his half-share of the business. Today, Dean was a multimillionaire entrepreneur who owned a national office-cleaning franchise. The lad from the rough council estate laughed as he told Pete about his good fortune.

Pete changed the subject. 'What are you doin' here, then?' he asked. Dean told him that he had been visiting LIPA to see about setting up an endowment fund at the Institute, to give some talented but underprivileged student the chance to make a career in music.

'I wanted to give somethin' back to the city, like. I mean I've got more money than I know what to do with and me accountant says I might as well give some of it to a worthy cause, otherwise the tax man'll grab it, just like George Harrison said in that song what he wrote, back in the sixties. It was Macca who suggested the idea when he came round to my place for dinner the other week. I've got loads of contacts in the music business.'

Dean looked at his watch. 'In fact, I'm just off now to see if I can help a guy with a little problem he's got. He's the entertainment officer on one of them cruise ships. Roger, his name is; I met him through his wife, a couple of years back. Nice girl she was, very friendly, like, if you know what I mean.'

He told Pete that there was a job going for a musician on the *Black Knight* which, following a severe outbreak of Norovirus, the tabloids had maliciously renamed the 'Black Death'. Dean's friend Roger desperately needed a replacement for their star turn, a singer who hadn't recovered from the illness in time for the next cruise which was due to be leaving Liverpool a couple of days later.

'It'd be money for old rope for some lucky sod,' said Dean. 'All you've got to do is sing for a couple of hours or so each evening. You get free board and lodging and all the booze you can handle. It'd be a bit like the old days. I'd love to do it, get back to me roots, like, but I don't reckon the wife would be too keen on me clearin' off for months at a time. It'd be just up your street, Pete. Still, I don't suppose you'd be interested in that sort of gig, what with you being famous after the Eurovision and everything.'

Pete swallowed hard. 'Well, Dean, as it happens, I'm at a bit of a loose end at the moment. It sounds like it could be interesting.'

His former band-mate looked at him, appraisingly. 'Tell you what, then,' said Dean, 'How's about I give me mate a bell and set up a meeting? You can take it from there.'

Thirty-six

Anyone in search of a symbol of American 'get up and go' needed to look no further than the *Black Knight*'s multi-billionaire American owner, Cheeseman 'Cheddar' Nimrods Jr. Immensely proud of his dirt-poor origins in a small Arkansas town, where his family regarded the trailer trash as the local gentry, 'Cheddar' – nobody who wished to remain in his employment called him by his given name - began his pursuit of the American Dream at the age of seven by making clothes pegs by hand and selling them to the neighbourhood gypsies.

Cheddar's next idea was, as he himself often said, divinely inspired. On Sunday mornings he would stand outside the doors of the local church as the congregants emerged after the service. Spiritually uplifted, they could not resist feeling pity for the doleful young ragamuffin who, with tears in his eyes, asked them most respectfully if they could possibly let him have any garments that they no longer needed so that he could give them to his poor widowed mother and his six siblings.

Predictably, none of the congregants had any unwanted clothing about their person. Instead they would invariably give him a few dollars which Cheddar pocketed with tearful mumbles of gratitude. His benefactors might have been less charitably inclined had they known that the boy's tears were caused by a slice of raw onion judiciously concealed in a bandaged hand with which from time to time he dabbed his eyes.

The budding entrepreneur invested wisely the money he was given. For a token one dollar he acquired a struggling local free newspaper which he soon made profitable by selling advertising space at irresistible rates. For those of his customers whose grasp of English was tenuous, the enterprising youth offered – for a fee, naturally - to draft advertisements for their products.

Cheddar experienced a temporary setback, however, when he sought to expand his interests; on submitting a self-publicising advertorial to the *National Enquirer,* the editor rejected the text on the grounds that it lacked credibility and was in extremely bad taste.

The young man, however, refused to be put off; by the age of thirty Cheddar had amassed a huge fortune, founded on the acquisition of local, then regional, then national newspapers.

His keen eye for a bargain led him across the Atlantic where he snapped up one of the oldest journals in Fleet Street, the old-established but debt-mired *Daily Excess*.

Boundlessly enthusiastic about expanding and diversifying his commercial portfolio, Cheddar Nimrods used his connections in the UK to target potential clients back home, via the *Excess's* American sister paper, the coast-to-coast daily *Federal and Regional Telegraph*.

The Fart, as the newspaper was popularly known, followed assiduously the journalistic principle of never overestimating its readership. Within a few years it became the most widely read publication in the entire United States. As well as presenting its readers with stories and features which made those featured in the *National Enquirer* seem paragons of plausibility, the Fart advertised exciting voyages of discovery aboard Nimrods' luxury cruise ship the *Black Knight*, an elderly, converted car-ferry which he had saved from the breaker's yard and bought for a nominal sum of one cent.

Nimrods' most popular offer was a week's "heritage cruise" around the British Isles. The highlights were day-long stops at Cardiff, Dover, Hull, Edinburgh, Belfast, Dublin and Liverpool. His clients would go off on day trips in search of their ancestry before embarking on the week-long journey back across the 'pond' to their home port of Miami.

*

When Pete turned up at the Liverpool cruise terminal, he was greeted enthusiastically by Roger, the *Black Knight*'s Entertainment Officer.

'Mr Wasserman,' he gushed, 'or may I call you Pete? First of all let me tell you how delighted we are to welcome such a famous artiste as yourself on board the *Black Knight*. You'll be in excellent company: we have the man who played tambourine in Elvis's band when he did his famous comeback tour in sixty-eight, and there's also the girl who was one of the backing singers on the Everly Brothers' very last single before they split up, back in the early seventies.'

Roger, who was about the same age as Pete, cleared his throat.

'There's just one more thing I have to mention,' he continued. He sounded embarrassed. 'I'm quite sure that the matter won't arise, but I am required to inform you nevertheless, just for the record. There are strict rules prohibiting any form of, er, inappropriate fraternisation between the ship's staff and our guests.'

Roger noticed that Pete looked puzzled. 'That is to say,' he elaborated, 'members of the crew are not permitted to enter the cabin of any passenger. Or vice versa. I'm sure you'll understand. Anyway,' Roger continued hurriedly, 'enough of that. Let me show you round the ship and introduce you to the other members of our little company. On the *Black Knight* we members of the entertainment staff like to think of ourselves as one big happy family. Speaking of which, let me introduce you to my wife, Sharon. '

The Entertainment Officer's wife was much younger than her husband. An attractive red-head, she smiled at Pete and shook his hand for a second or two longer than mere courtesy required.

'I'm delighted to meet you,' she said. 'I loved your song, *Tina*; it was so sad. Did you write it for someone special?'

Before Pete could reply, her husband continued: 'Sorry, darling; there are a few things that Pete and I have to sort out before the passengers start to come back on board. He'll want to see the facilities and also where he'll be sleeping. Oh yes, and of course,' he added with a little laugh, 'all the places on the ship where he'll be performing.'

*

The *Black Knight*, as well as having made the news as a health hazard, was notorious throughout the cruise ship entertainment community as the graveyard of show biz has-beens. Among these was an ageing Canadian with a grey ponytail who had played rhythm guitar in a one-hit-wonder band in the mid-sixties, a cross-eyed Welsh opera singer who had finished third in a long-forgotten TV talent show, and a Bulgarian former trainee ballet dancer whose body had developed far too much for her to be aerodynamically viable. She was, however, very popular, especially with those male members of the entertainment staff who were not gay.

Pete's fellow entertainers took to him straightaway; they could see that he was an ordinary bloke, just like them - no airs and graces. Pete quickly took to shipboard life, too. He didn't mind the poky cabin he had been given in the bowels of the ship; he had got used to living in cramped conditions in the flat with Tina. The prospect of having a nice long lie-in in the mornings appealed to him and he had been told that all his meals would be provided. He would even get his clothes washed and ironed for free.

As far as the workload was concerned, Dean had been dead right. All Pete had to do each day was to play three sessions in the late afternoon and evening, rotating between the various lounges and bars.

He never had to buy a drink; many of the women passengers asked him to pose for a photograph with them. Some of them, made daring by one more cocktail than was good for them, put their arm behind him and squeezed his behind while their unsuspecting husbands fiddled with their cameras. When they had finished snapping away they would buy Pete a drink to thank him for graciously consenting to be photographed with their wives.

Pete had brought his Clavinova onboard. Its electronic database now contained a huge selection of music from the sixties, complete with full backing and harmony vocal tracks. The repertoire of mainly sad country and western songs appealed in particular to the passengers, especially the female ones, when they had become sentimental after a few drinks.

The artistes' performance schedule was organised by Sharon; Pete's free time coincided with her husband's lengthy periods on duty. Much to her disappointment, however, Pete did not take the hint.

She told Pete that he would receive a percentage of the bar takings and gave him a useful tip: 'Remember to tell the punters that the more they drink, the better you sound!' Each night, when the audience was well oiled, he finished his last set playing *Tina* on his ukulele. The applause was always rapturous.

*

Pete had attracted a steadily growing band of admirers. As he was packing away his ukulele after one late night session, an elderly American came up to him.

'Say, Pete, where did you get that family name, Wasserman, from? It sure don't sound British to me.'

Pete told him briefly about his family background, how in 1943 his father, a Luftwaffe pilot, had become a prisoner of war after his plane had been shot down after veering off course. He explained that his mother, who worked at a biscuit factory near her home in Stockport, had fallen in love with the handsome young German POW while he was working there under supervision, and how, even though Pete's dad was an amiable, decidedly non-Nazi, the hostile attitude of their neighbours had made the couple decide to move to Liverpool to make a fresh start.

'Geez, that's a real awesome story!' exclaimed the American. 'My own family history is kindalike real interesting, too.' He proceeded to treat Pete to a detailed account of his own ancestry. Twenty minutes later he looked at Pete triumphantly.

'So, I guess I got English, Scottish, Irish *and* Welsh blood in me. What do you think about *that*, huh?'

Pete had found the American's story fascinating and offered him his opinion:

'It sounds like your mam was a right goer.'

*

During the days when the *Black Knight* was in port, Pete had no commitments and was free to do as he pleased. As a solo act, he didn't need to rehearse; he was quite content to seek out a quiet corner on the top deck near the buffet restaurant and while away the hours with a beer or two. He watched as clinically obese passengers waddled along in search of food. Having succeeded in their mission they waddled past him again. In one podgy hand they held plates heaped precariously high with pizza and fries; in the other, as a concession to healthy eating, they clutched a can of diet Coke. Above one man's distended belly, the legend on the overstretched, ketchup-stained T shirt proclaimed: 'Small is beautiful'.

Around the ship, Pete noticed lots of odd-looking couples. The men were old, at least seventy-five he reckoned. The least doddery of them got around with the aid of a walking stick, the more decrepit shuffled along using a zimmerframe. Each, to Pete's amazement, seemed to be accompanied by a slim woman who looked many years younger than her companion. The women's faces, he thought, looked as if they had been freshly ironed. He noticed, too, that they never laughed or even smiled. It was only when he saw them at closer range that he realised that the women were much older than they looked; no amount of cosmetic procedures could hide the tell-tale liver spots on the backs of their hands, or the corrugated folds of skin at their throats.

*

The crew of the *Black Knight* had nicknamed the ship's casino 'Death Valley'; deserted by day, noisy and nicotine-filled by night, it was frequented mainly by elderly, unaccompanied chain-smokers. While waiting for cancer or cirrhosis to claim them, they spent their remaining days and dollars relentlessly feeding coins by the bucketful into the phalanx of slot machines. When, every so often, one of them spewed out a jingling cascade of coins, the features of the gamblers betrayed no emotion.

As Pete was walking through the casino one evening to prepare for his next set in the piano bar, he noticed a very large blonde woman with Slavonic features who was sitting on a stool in front of one of the slot machines. He had a vague idea that he had seen her before, somewhere. When Pete asked one of the croupiers who she was, he learned that she, also, was one of the entertainers on the *Black Knight*. Sitting in front of a one-armed bandit, she hummed a familiar tune.

Pete recognised the melody. Sensing that she was being stared at, the woman looked up from her bucket and her eyes met Pete's. She scowled and started to mutter angrily. It was then that Pete remembered where he had seen her before: she was the one who, mouthing imprecations in her native language, had stormed off the stage during the auditions in Bograd when Pete had heard her appalling rendition of *Moon River*.

Thirty-seven

Each day Pete looked forward to the ship putting into port so that he could send a postcard to Tina. One day, when he phoned her on a whim, she told him that she was doing okay and had got herself a nice little part-time job in a betting shop. She also told him that she was 'seeing someone'.

'He's a widower,' she explained. 'I met him at the local hospice. I help out there a couple of days each week. My friend June is a volunteer there as well. She still works on the check-out at Tesco's. She introduced him to me.'

'I'm pleased for you, Tina,' said Pete. 'No, I really am. You deserve to be happy. I'm just sorry that it couldn't be with me.' Unable to think of anything else to say, he mumbled goodbye and hung up.

*

He had a look at the ship's daily information leaflet to see if there was anything interesting he could find to do to pass the time before his first set of the evening. There was a talk by one of the entertainment staff about shopping opportunities at the next port of call. Tina would have liked that, he thought. A guest speaker from an American university was scheduled to deliver a lecture on the rise, decline and fall of the British Empire. There was a table tennis competition, a tutorial on the art of napkin-folding and a once-in-a-lifetime opportunity to buy silver and gold chains by the inch.

One afternoon, a few days after he had joined the *Black Knight*, Pete noticed at the bottom of the daily leaflet that there was a meeting at four o'clock for 'Friends of Bill'. 'Who's this Bill geezer?' he wondered. 'He must have loads of friends if there's a party just for him.' He looked at his watch; it was coming up to a quarter past four. As he had nothing better to do, he thought that he would go along to the party just to see what was going on. On the way he stopped off at one of the bars and picked up a can of lager to take with him. He was getting used to the layout of the ship and soon found the room where the meeting was taking place. The sign on the door invited Bill's friends to come right on in. Pete turned the handle and entered.

Heads turned to look at him and, scowling, immediately turned away again. He could hear angry muttering. Pete took a swig of lager from the can. The muttering grew louder. A waiter carrying a tray laden with glasses of fruit juice came up to him.

'I'm sorry, sir, alcohol is not permitted at this party.'

'What d'yer mean?' asked Pete, aghast at the very idea. 'I thought that Bill would be celebrating, like it's his birthday or something.'

The waiter whispered in his ear: 'This is a meeting for *Friends – of - Bill'*. Pete's face showed no trace of comprehension. The waiter tried again. 'There's no booze because it's for members of AA.'

Pete was even more perplexed. 'Why do they want to have a meeting for the AA when they're on a fuckin' ship?' he asked. 'It's not like there's any cars on board!'

The waiter whispered again: 'It's not *the* AA, it's just AA. Friends of Bill, it's like a secret code; this is a meeting for members of Alcoholics Anonymous.'

*

The following day the latest issue of *What's on around the ship* informed passengers that, in addition to an exciting deck quoits competition whose winner would receive a fabulous prize, a Bridge seminar for advanced players and a 'get by in Gaelic' lesson, there would be a meeting that afternoon in for 'Friends of Dorothy'.

That looks a bit more promising, thought Pete; there'll probably be loads of unattached birds there. He decided, in view of his misunderstanding over the friends of Bill, that it might be better not to go to the meeting with a drink in his hand.

The meeting was in Giovanni's Room, one of the venues where he performed each evening. When he went in, Pete was disappointed to see that there were no women there. Everyone seemed to be in couples, though. A young man detached himself from the companion with whom he had been talking and came over to speak to him.

'Hell-*o*!' said the young man, smiling. 'I've seen you around the ship and I've caught your act in here. When you sang *Tina* I thought to myself what a lovely song! It's so *tragic.* I would never have guessed that you were one of us.'

It was then that Pete realised he had made another mistake.

*

A few days later, while the *Black Knight* was moored at South Queensferry, Pete was feeling more bored than usual. Nearly all the passengers had gone ashore. Some had opted for a sight-seeing excursion to Edinburgh, organised by Roger. Others, more ambitiously, had set off by themselves on a pilgrimage to some obscure hamlet or other in the hope of discovering their family origins.

As Pete wandered round the virtually deserted ship, he came across a young man in uniform who was tapping gently, in what appeared to be a pre-arranged code, on the door of one of the staterooms. Almost immediately the door opened and the man went in. A few seconds later, a woman's arm emerged and hung up a 'do not disturb' sign.

*

The same evening Pete had just finished one of his sets and was having a quiet drink when Sharon came and sat down next to him.

'I get really bored when we're at sea,' she complained. 'There's absolutely nothing to do all day and of course Roger is so busy all the time, what with organising the shows and chatting with the passengers and taking them on excursions. I hardly ever see him. Sometimes I get very lonely.' She looked at Pete. 'Don't you get lonely, too?'

*

On the last night of the cruise, after he had finished his final set of the evening, Pete was having a drink by himself after the last of his elderly female admirers had gone. The blonde from Bograd was there, too, but was studiously ignoring him. Sharon came up to the bar and sat on the stool next to him.

'I've been watching you perform, Pete. You probably didn't notice me. I always sit right at the back of the room, away from all the others.' She leaned over to him; he could smell her perfume. 'I think you're very talented. Most of the acts that Roger signs up for this rust bucket are third rate. But you're different; what you do, it's really special. Your voice is very romantic, but so sad.' She looked into his eyes. 'Would you like to come back to my room for a nightcap? Roger won't be off duty for ages.'

*

The Entertainment Officer had been tipped off about what his wife was up to by the spurned blonde from Slavonicia, who was bent on revenge. When Pete and Sharon had gone off together, she had seen her opportunity. As she fancied Roger as much as she hated Pete, it was a perfect opportunity for her to kill two birds with one stone. She watched with a look of smug satisfaction as Roger opened the stateroom door and burst in. Pete and Sharon were caught *in flagrante.* Her husband looked at them in astonishment.

'What the hell do you think you're doing?' he shouted.

His wife, unperturbed, turned to Pete:

'See? I told you he was stupid.'

Thirty-eight

Early the following morning, Pete found himself back on shore again, jobless and, now that the bank had taken away his house, homeless. His only remaining possession was his old ukulele. The last thing he saw as he was put ashore in Liverpool was his Clavinova being smashed to pieces by the Entertainments Officer, aided enthusiastically by the vengeful blonde. Sharon was nowhere to be seen.

Dishevelled and unshaven, he wandered around for an hour or so before finding himself in the city centre, near Lime Street station. Pedestrians, frowning at the bedraggled wreck walking towards them, gave him a wide berth. It wasn't all that long ago, he thought, that some of these same people would have been cheering his name, celebrating his success.

The lyrics of an old blues number came into his head. Suddenly he had an idea. He remembered seeing a TV programme a few years earlier featuring a now internationally famous singer who had started out as a busker, entertaining the crowds outside West End theatres in London. It was worth a try; he had nothing more to lose.

Pete ambled onto the station concourse and stood near the platform entrance. He checked his ukulele to make sure that it was in tune. He had played only a few chords when he realised that he didn't have a receptacle for any loose change that people might want to give him. He rummaged in a litter bin and found a paper cup. He put it down on the ground in front of him and started to strum again.

The lyrics of 'Nobody knows you when you're down and out' were depressingly apposite. After playing for twenty minutes, all Pete had to show for his efforts was a ten pence piece which an old lady had thrown, inaccurately, in the direction of the cup.

A young police constable came up to him.

'Do you have a permit for busking, sir?' he enquired politely.

Pete was about to explain his situation when a stray mongrel, which had been wandering aimlessly around the station, came over to where he was standing. The animal cocked a rear leg and with uncanny accuracy directed a stream of urine into the cup. Its duty done, the dog wandered off. Pete sensed that his career as a busker was over.

There was just one person left, he thought, who might be able to help him. Pete started to walk quickly in the direction of the Griffin. Bert, the landlord, had always been sympathetic. Maybe he'd be able to find him a job. Anything would do, just until he got back on his feet again.

*

Pete was in luck. As he was about to push the heavy swing door of the pub, it opened outward of its own accord. A scrawny lad made a rapid exit, propelled by one of Bert's size eleven shoes.

'And don't let me catch you in here again, yer thievin' little bugger,' roared Bert, 'or I'll have the bizzies on yer!'

Bert hadn't seen Pete, who followed him back to the bar. 'Hi, Bert!' he said. 'How's things?'

The landlord, breathing hard from his exertions, seemed pleased to see him.

'Hello, Pete! What're you doin' round here? I thought you'd be tourin' or somethin', makin' a mint, like.'

Pete gave Bert an edited version of what had happened since the song contest.

'So,' he concluded, 'I was wonderin' if you could, yer know, give us a bed for a couple of nights?'

'Tell you what,' said Bert. He wanted to help Pete and business had been very slow recently; maybe having him around would help trade to pick up. 'I'll give yer a billet if you'll sing here a couple of nights a week. What d'yer say?'

Pete thought it over for about a tenth of a second before replying: 'Yer gorra deal!'

Thirty-nine

The proud boast of the *Sunday Planet* was that, unlike its frivolous and superficial competitors, it got right down to the bottom of things. It adopted an equally fundamental approach to the photographs it published; the tabloid's most popular feature was the 'rear without peer', for which a seemingly endless number of young women happily posed.

One of these, while chatting with one of the paper's reporters who had come along to gather a few titbits of information about her to print alongside the photograph, casually let slip that she was the granddaughter of Pete Wasserman. 'Oh, really?' asked the reporter, sceptically.

'Yeah, it's true, honest,' said the girl. 'My gran used to live in Liverpool when she was about the same age as what I am now. She went out with Pete a couple of times. She'd seen him when he was playing with a band and she fancied him. She didn't know anything about, yer know, contraception and all that sort of thing. She only did it with him the once, she said, but she got herself pregnant. She had to leave school and everything. She never told Pete about it or nothin'; he was only a young lad himself, she said, so there was no point. My mam says that gran was always telling her to be careful when she went out with a boy because they were only interested in one thing.'

'How old's your mam, then, if you don't mind me asking?' enquired the reporter, who now seemed much more interested.

'She's thirty-six, almost thirty-seven; it's her birthday next week,' she replied. 'I don't know what to get her for a prezzy. Got any ideas?'

'Not a clue, love, but this may help you to get something nice.' He took a fifty pound note from his wallet and slipped it into her bikini bottom. 'Thanks very much, you've been very helpful. By the way, just out of interest, how old are you?'

'Nearly twenty,' she said, proudly. The reporter laughed.

'I reckon your gran knew what she was talking about, but I'm glad your mam didn't pay any attention.'

*

One Monday morning Tanya arrived for work as usual at her office in central London, just off Park Lane. Efficient and hard-working, she had been in her present job for eight years, since graduating with a first in Psychology from Cambridge.

That morning's commute had been even more unpleasant than usual; she had had to stand for the entire hour-long journey from her flat in a distant suburb of North-West London with her face only inches away from the armpit of a young man who was evidently a stranger to deodorant. Several minutes after getting off the tube she could still smell his sweat.

Passing through the automatic double doors of the modern office block, she showed her security pass to the uniformed concierge who smiled and wished her good morning.

The young woman took the lift up to the top floor offices of the internationally renowned publicist Cliff Maxford. She hung up her coat on a hook on the back of the door and turned on her computer. As she waited for it to fire up, she cast a glance at the telephone hub. The red light indicating that voicemail messages had been received over the weekend was flashing. Another collection of idiots and time wasters, she thought. With a sigh, she pressed the 'play' button.

The first two messages were barely coherent; both were from a neurotic teenage actress, a bit part player in a daytime soap on a cable channel, who claimed that she had been made pregnant by a TV star who was a household name. The fucking bastard – the convent-educated Tanya winced as she listened to the shrill diatribe - had refused to admit responsibility and she now wanted Cliff Maxford's help in exposing him as a philanderer.

There was only one small problem with the woman's story; to Tanya's certain knowledge, the alleged inseminator was gay. The actress, well known for being indiscriminate with her favours, was simply making a very clumsy attempt to gain some free publicity. Tanya sighed again as she deleted the first two messages.

The third was from a woman who spoke with a strong Liverpool accent; she stated in a perfectly calm voice that, as a consequence of a one-night stand by her mother in the early sixties, she was Pete Wasserman's secret love child and that this might be of interest to Mr Maxford.

Tanya had developed over the years a nose for a promising story. Silently, she mouthed to her boss who, as usual, was on the telephone: 'Cliff, I think you should listen to this.' Maxford trusted Tanya's judgment. He ended his call as soon as he could and came over to her desk to listen to the recording.

Cliff Maxford had built a highly successful and lucrative career selling titillating stories to an ever-increasing number of downmarket publications, all intent on outbidding their rivals in their public-spirited quest to expose the libidinous and/or pharmaceutical excesses of the rich and famous. He never ceased to marvel at the public's seemingly inexhaustible appetite for the revelations of publicity-hungry wannabees. He was amused by the airbrushed photos and juvenile prose churned out by these publications but he refused to be judgmental; it would be stupid, after all, to bite the hand that fed him so well. He played the message again.

The woman, unlike the earlier caller, refused to disclose any further information about her identity; all she was willing to say was that her name began with P. She provided her mobile number and said that she knew several other women who had a similar story to tell.

Cliff Maxford was used to such initial reluctance on the part of people who contacted his office. Nearly all of them were women, most of them young enough to be his daughter. Or even in some cases, he reflected ruefully as the years went by ever faster, his granddaughter. His sympathetic approach helped him to win the confidence of even the most reticent of those who contacted him. He knew that, eventually, they would reveal to him their most intimate secrets.

Cliff cancelled his appointments for the rest of the day; there was nothing in his schedule that he could not confidently delegate to one of his junior colleagues. This was one story that he definitely wanted to handle himself.

'Miss Hyde,' he said to Tanya with mock formality, 'please would you get me P's number?'

The phone was answered on the first ring. Cliff smiled; it was obvious that the woman was anxious to unburden herself. He knew from experience that it was going to be a long but, with any luck, a very rewarding day.

*

Three days after the mysterious P had contacted Cliff Maxford, there appeared in the *Planet* a huge photo of Pete above the headline: 'Pete Wossadad!' There followed lurid details about five women, all in their mid to late thirties, who claimed that Pete Wasserman was their father.

It was Bert, the landlord of the Griffin, who showed Pete the story. Pete shook his head and smiled.

'Not a cat in hell's chance, mate,' he said. 'I had a lot of birds back in them days, but I always took precautions.' He smiled ruefully, remembering the dose he had caught when he had just been starting his sexual education. The treatment at the pox hospital had not been pleasant; since then he had been careful to have a packet of johnnies with him. The only time he had slipped up was when he had taken Tina for a drive in the countryside, all those years before. The events of that evening had taken both of them by surprise.

Forty

As Pete was coming out of a pub a couple of months later after a lunchtime pint with a couple of old friends he turned round to say goodbye. Not looking where he was going, he collided with a suntanned and elegantly-dressed woman. Weighed down by several designer store shopping bags, she stumbled, her purchases scattering over the pavement.

'Sorry, luv,' said Pete, instinctively. 'Lemme 'elp yer.'

The woman was in her fifties, but looked quite a lot younger. As she crouched down by his side, each of them stretched out a hand simultaneously towards the same bag, their faces only inches apart. The woman looked closely at him.

'It's not you, is it? Pete?'

Pete looked at her, wondering where he had seen her before.

'It's Maggie. From Warrington? We went out together a couple of times. Mind you, it was a long time ago, back in the sixties - sixty-two I think it was - when I was still at school. You used to be in that group, didn't you? I can't remember now what you were called. We all thought you were fab!'

She looked at him and giggled as her teenage memories came into sharper focus. 'You must have gone out with loads of girls back then, so I can understand if you don't remember me. But I certainly remember *you*! Tell you what, why don't we meet up for lunch? How about tomorrow? It'll be my treat.'

*

The following day they met for lunch at the Adelphi Hotel in the city centre.

'Well, Pete,' said Maggie, taking a sip of her skinny latte after picking at her *salade niçoise*, 'it looks like you've come a long way since the old days. You're quite a star, now! It doesn't surprise me, though; I knew even then that you had something special. I suppose you've been in the music industry all these years?' she continued. 'Living the high life, I'll bet!'

Pete thought it best not to mention Tina, the succession of low-paid jobs and the tiny flat he had shared with his long-suffering wife. Quickly, he changed the subject and asked Maggie what she'd been up to since their fling all those years before.

'Well,' said Maggie, 'around that time I managed to get myself pregnant.' She saw the question beginning to form on Pete's lips. 'Don't worry,' she reassured him, 'I don't *think* it was yours. Anyway, I got married when I was seventeen. He was quite a bit older than me. I was far too young, but in my position I didn't have much choice. He was nearly always away on business. I didn't have a clue what sort of work he did. I still don't! Anyway, surprise, surprise, the marriage didn't last. So there I was, nineteen years old, divorced and on my own again. And of course, there was Petra, too.'

Pete looked at her enquiringly.

'Petra, my little girl,' explained Maggie. 'Well, she's not so little now. We don't see much of one another these days. She doesn't approve of Henry. And *he* can't stand *her*, either. He told her he's not going to give her a penny when he pops off. Can't say I blame him; after all, she's not *his* child, is she? Anyway, where was I? Oh yes. My daddy took my ex to the cleaner's.' Noticing Pete's questioning look, she added. 'Oh, I didn't say, did I? Daddy was a solicitor – he made sure I got the house and the car and quite a bit of money.' She smiled at him sweetly. 'Who said marriage isn't worthwhile?'

'So what are you doing now?' asked Pete, grateful that Tina wasn't there to hear their conversation.

'Oh, didn't I mention it?' she replied, 'I'm getting married again in a few weeks' time. That's why I had all those bags when you bumped into me! I'd been in town getting some things for my going away outfit after the wedding.' The words kept tumbling out. 'He's really quite a sweetie, is Henry,' she added, 'and very generous, too.'

Delving into her Gucci handbag she produced a photograph of herself with the man she was going to marry. Pete thought for a second or two that he had seen him before, somewhere, before dismissing the idea; it was impossible - he didn't move in the same circles as Henry.

'Of course,' continued Maggie, 'he's quite a lot older than me, and at his age he's not looking for, you know... He's been retired for quite a few years and he's been very lonely since his wife died last year. We met on the Internet. He's absolutely *loaded*! He owns this fantastic country house hotel in Cheshire. It used to belong to a Duke or a Count or someone like that. The place is *hundreds* of years old. It was almost in ruins when Henry bought it for a song a couple of years ago and had it done up. Anyway, last month some mega hotel chain based in South East Asia made him an offer he couldn't refuse.' Maggie giggled. 'It sounds like something out of *The Godfather*, doesn't it?! I said to him: Henry, before you sell the hotel, we absolutely *must* have our wedding there!'

She took another sip of coffee and turned to Pete. An idea had just occurred to her.

'I know it's a terrible cheek, Pete, and I know how busy you must be, but I was just wondering ... would you be able to come and sing a couple of songs at the reception after our wedding? Just for old times' sake? It would really make my day.'

*

On the day of Maggie's nuptials, Pete turned up early at the Nanchester Hall Country Hotel. The young woman at the reception desk was busy attending to other wedding guests so he decided to have a nose around and see what the place was like. Perhaps he'd be able to find somewhere to change into his stage clothes. He went down a corridor and tried the doors of several rooms; all of them were locked. Pete turned a corner and tried another door. This time the handle turned. In front of a full length mirror stood Maggie, resplendent in a white silk dressing gown. When she saw him in the mirror, the scream that she was about to emit froze on her lips and changed into a huge smile.

'It's just like old times, Pete!' she said.

Ancient feelings resurfaced.

*

As Maggie walked down the aisle to be united with her bridegroom, everyone remarked on how radiant she was looking. There was a glow on her cheeks, and her eyes were sparkling. Pete was standing at the end of a row of seats. As she passed him she whispered: 'I'm so glad you could come.'

At the reception, Pete sang a few songs, including an old hit from the sixties, *I can't let Maggie go.* Henry was effusive in his gratitude:

'Thank you so much for performing for Maggie' - he paused to correct himself - 'I mean for my wife,' he said coyly. 'Having you here has really made her day.'

Pete thought that Henry's voice seemed familiar. Suddenly he remembered where he had encountered Maggie's new husband. The words that the elderly man in front of him was now uttering were somewhat different from those Pete had heard him use when they had last met. Henry had been chairman of the magistrates before whom Pete, many years earlier, had appeared on a number of occasions charged with being drunk and disorderly.

Forty-one

Late one chilly, drizzly morning, the phone rang at the Griffin. Bert answered. It was a bad line.

'Is possibility speak to Pete Wasserman, please?' enquired a woman's voice.

'Hang on a minute, love, I'll see if he's up yet,' replied the landlord.

Pete had just surfaced with a hangover after his performance in the lounge bar the night before. He had been a great success; it had required a considerable effort to finish all the drinks he'd been bought. He picked up the phone.

'Pete here,' he said. 'Who's that?'

'I thanking my goodness I find you!'

As soon as he heard the idiosyncratic English, he knew who it was.

Excitedly Irena told Pete about her meteoric rise in the Ministry of "Cool-toor".

'I going to be hostess for Eurovision Song Contest this year in Bograd.'

'That's great, Irena!' said Pete. 'Who's going to be performing for Slavonicia?'

Irena laughed. 'The President has decide that our country will not enter the contest this time. Not never again. He say it would be unpossible to find better singer than you. So – how do you say - we quit while we are ahead. But silly I! I am nearly forgetful of the most important thing! Our President has ask me to invite you to come to Slavonicia as his honourable guest.'

'Sounds great,' said Pete, 'when does he want me to come?'

Irena paused. For a moment Pete thought the line had gone dead. After a few moments she spoke:

'I am already up in the air in the President's private jet. We will arriving at Liverpool airport in approximatively one hour. Can you come back with me to Bograd tonight?'

*

There was a third passenger on the flight back to Bograd. President Sonofábic had also invited the recently ennobled Douglas, Lord Anstruther of Strathmiglo, to spend a few days as his guest.

The President was doubly grateful; not only had the diplomat extricated his errant daughter Petrushka from a situation which could well have had damaging implications for his presidency, his friend Douglas had also arranged for him to receive, in conditions of total secrecy, a regular supply of stimulating substances from South America.

Thirty thousand feet above central Europe, Pete sank back into the plush leather recliner chair, sipped the coffee thoughtfully provided by Irena and listened to Lord Anstruther.

The noble Lord's expression was one of deep concern. He was, he said, most distressed to hear of Pete's recent misfortunes. 'Perhaps I may be able to be of some assistance?' he ventured. 'Your undoubted talent deserves to be more widely appreciated. I think that I might be able to arrange something suitable.'

*

233

As Pete emerged from the plane, he was greeted by masses of Slavonician citizens waving Union flags in one hand and the country's national standard - its motif was an axe cleaving a beetroot - in the other. The crowds lined the newly constructed six-lane Wasserman Way which led from Bograd International Airport to the centre of the capital. As the limousine carrying Pete, Lord Anstruther and Irena drew to a halt, the Head of State descended the steps of the Presidential Palace in the newly renamed Peter Wassermanstrat to embrace in one of his famous bear-hugs the saviour of the nation.

Forty-two

Reclining on her *chaise longue*, Lady Anstruther was once again locked in her daily struggle with the *Telegraph* cryptic crossword as the television murmured in the background. Suddenly, an excited announcement broke her concentration:

'Sky! - first with the news, wherever and whenever it breaks. We're going over now to our News Editor, Ruby Leaky. Ruby...'

'Yes, for once it is *good* news that is making the headlines!' she intoned, in characteristically breathless style. 'In what has been hailed as a major scientific breakthrough, food technologists from the UK and the People's Independent State of Slavonicia have confirmed that a special strain of beetroot, which forms the basis of the Slavonician diet and is to be found only in that country, possesses significant health benefits. Apparently the beetroot, when liquidised but not allowed to ferment, produces unusually high levels of energy in those who consume it. Only last month, a new terminal was constructed at Bograd International Airport in record time. It is claimed that the project was completed so quickly as a result of workers being given large quantities of the miracle health drink, which enabled them to work longer, harder and faster.

'I understand from informed sources that plans are already at an advanced stage to process, under licence, the massive over-production of Slavonicia's beetroot crop which, until recently, had been used principally in the production of vodka. Unlike alcohol, however, the beetroot-based drink is non-addictive.

'A multi-billion pound scheme, financed by the European Community, has been set up to produce the life-enhancing beverage and will be administered by the newly-formed joint Anglo-Slavonician Council for Health and Nutrition. Plans to export this revolutionary energy drink are due to be announced later today.

'In a further development, Slavonicia's application to become the latest member state of the European Community is to be decided shortly. The Council's President, the UK's Lord An ...'

It was getting late. Lady Anstruther's unsuccessful attempt to stifle a yawn caused her to miss the reference to her husband. All she knew was that, once again, he was out of the country engaged on some business to do with Europe. She really wasn't interested.

She looked at the TV listings and flicked the remote. A re-run of an old episode of *Neighbours* filled the screen. With a sigh of contentment, she once again admitted defeat by the crossword and settled down to watch Kylie Minogue and Jason Donovan. As far as she was concerned, TV was much more interesting than all that boring old politics.

*

Beetroot was most definitely not on the menu at the banquet hosted at the Presidential Palace by President Sonovábic. The guest of honour, Pete Wasserman, was invested by the beaming Head of State as an Honorary Son of the Nation.

Lord Anstruther had also been invited. President Sonofábic's recently acquired taste for Scottish cuisine was evident from the menu that he had devised for his guests. The banquet included deep-fried haggis and, in recognition of Pete's extraordinary contribution to the nation, a signature dish of scouse.

The Scot took another sip of Glenfarclas – the President's planning had been as meticulous as usual - put down his glass and stood up to speak. After expressing the usual courtesies, he paused and looked round the room at the distinguished company. It was clear to everyone present that what he was about to say was to be momentous. Smiling broadly, he turned to his host. Irena stood by the diplomat's side, ready to translate his words into her native tongue, for the benefit of the many non-English speakers present.

'I am delighted, Mr President,' he began, turning to his new friend and ally, 'to be the bearer of what I am sure you will agree with me is excellent news. At an extraordinary meeting of the Heads of State of the European Union which I had the honour to chair, the application for membership of the Union by the People's Independent State of Slavonicia was approved unanimously.' As Irena conveyed the news, the room resonated to rapturous applause.

'Your nation,' continued Lord Anstruther, 'is extremely fortunate to be blessed with a forward-looking government under the inspirational leadership of President Sonofábic, who is truly' – he paused almost imperceptibly - 'a man of substance. Slavonicia has shown great courage in casting off the oppressive yoke of its unhappy recent past; your people have been liberated from political and economic slavery and your country is today a shining symbol of the happy marriage between socialism and free enterprise. I am certain that Slavonicia's long-overdue and most welcome membership of the European Community will herald a new age of peace and prosperity for us all.'

Lord Anstruther's speech continued in this vein for several minutes. He was well aware that the words tripping so effortlessly off his tongue were mere rhetoric, but they could not do any harm, he thought, in greasing the wheels of international diplomacy and co-operation.

*

Slavonicia was booming, both economically and sonically; in Bograd a major rebuilding programme of civic buildings had started, as had the construction of a country-wide network of six-lane motorways. It was rumoured that construction engineers were testing a new form of high explosive developed in the UK to enable them to tunnel through the granite mountain ranges to reach the country's flat central plains. The project, once completed, would provide high-speed links with the rest of Europe from which Slavonicia had been isolated economically as well as geographically throughout its long and unremarkable history.

Deep in the interior of the country, work was proceeding apace on what, according to unofficial leaks from NATO, appeared to be a military installation.

Forty-three

Lord Anstruther had had to return home immediately following the banquet, after receiving a panic-stricken phone call from the PM. It appeared that a front bench MP had been caught *in flagrante* with a bisexual rent boy and that one of the Sunday redtops had signalled its intention to publish full details of the scandal, complete with photographs. Perhaps, wondered the PM, Douglas might be able to use his contacts to keep the sordid business out of the papers. Douglas, after consulting his black book and making a single telephone call, was able to oblige.

*

After the banquet, Pete and Irena were invited by President Sonofábic to spend the rest of their stay in the Imperial suite on the top floor of the Presidential Palace

'How about it, Pete?' asked Irena, shyly. 'In our country, is law that no-one allowed to refuse invitation from President, or,' - she drew her hand rapidly across her throat - 'it is off with his head!'

'Bloody 'ell!' replied Pete, who had turned pale. 'That's a bit strong, but I reckon we'd better say yes.'

Irena, smiling, rolled her eyes and shook her head slowly in mock exasperation. 'Well, Pete; is that an invitation?' She took his hand. 'I was thinking you never going to ask!'

To Pete, holding Irena's hand felt perfectly natural. She led him slowly to the elevator.

*

Late in the morning of the fourth day of their holiday, there was a discreet knock at the door; it had slipped Pete's mind that Irena had asked the previous evening if it would be possible for them to have breakfast in bed as she was feeling rather tired. As Irena cracked open a rather runny boiled egg, her face turned a delicate shade of green. Clapping a hand over her mouth, she rushed to the bathroom.

'It's probably something you ate last night, luv,' said Pete through the bathroom door. When Irena emerged a few minutes later, her normal colour had returned and she was smiling.

Pete was relieved to see her looking better so quickly. 'Better out than in!' he quipped. Irena gave him a funny look.

'If you had followed that advice, I would not be feeling this way now,' she said, laughing. Irena's English was improving.

At first Pete looked puzzled; it took him a moment or two to work out what she meant. As he finally understood, a huge grin spread across his face.

*

President Sonofábic's daughter, having graduated with a First Class Honours degree, had now returned home to her proud father. His delight at her success was matched only by that of The Master of St Judas's. Shortly after the Conferring of Degrees ceremony, which the President had attended in a purely personal capacity, the newly ennobled Lord Blenkinsop of Oswaldtwistle had received a letter from the Department for Information, Culture and Knowledge informing him that his College, which he had feared would be a victim of the forthcoming Government spending cutbacks, was to be awarded a substantial grant in recognition of its outstanding contribution to the development of international relations.

*

On the morning of the last day of their stay at the Presidential Palace, the phone rang in Pete and Irena's suite as they were having breakfast. The caller was President Sonofábic.

'I wish to offer you, Mr Wasserman,' said without preamble the Head of State, 'the position of Senior Advisor for Popular Culture, a post which I have personally decided to create. You may be sure that the work you will be asked to perform will be of the highest importance and you will receive the eternal gratitude of the people of Slavonicia. Will you do me the honour of accepting?'

*

Three days a week, the new Senior Advisor for Popular Culture was chauffeured to his department at the Ministry to face the rigours of a four hour working day. After being driven home early each afternoon, Pete played happily in the large garden of the lakeside *dacha* that he shared with Irena and their little daughter, Gabrielle. In the skies high above their house could be seen the thin contrails of jet aircraft which had begun to fly, in increasing numbers, in and out of Bograd International Airport. There was increasing speculation in the Slavonician media that the airport was to be renamed in Pete's honour.

*

Irena had taken charge of Pete's liquid intake; every day she watched over him discreetly as he drank three large glasses of the beetroot-based potion which was rapidly gaining an international reputation as the elixir of life.

Pete featured prominently in a Pan-European multi-media advertising campaign which displayed images of him before and after his conversion from lager to the new wonder drink. Images of celebrity drug addicts and remorse-filled footballer philanderers were ousted from the front pages of celebrity magazines by the Eurovision winner's slimmed-down physique.

In television commercials, Pete sang *Tina,* for which new lyrics had been composed, extolling the beetroot beverage in several languages. The potion's phenomenal success had caused the share price of several multinational brewers to fall sharply.

Irena was happy, now that Pete was half the man he used to be. In the evenings, sitting on the front porch of their simply furnished but comfortable home, Pete liked nothing better than to take out his old, battered ukulele and serenade his wife as their little girl played contentedly.

Lightning Source UK Ltd.
Milton Keynes UK
UKOW050630051211

183222UK00001B/1/P

9 781908 481566